Midw

M000283324

Midwife to the Fairies

New and Selected Stories

Éilís Ní Dhuibhne

First published in 2003 by
Attic Press Ltd
Crawford Business Park
Crosses Green, Cork

Reprinted 2019

© Éilís Ní Dhuibhne 2003

The author has asserted her moral rights in this work.
All rights reserved. No part of this book may be reprinted or reproduced
or utilized in any electronic, mechanical or other means, now known or
hereafter invented, including photocopying or recording or otherwise,
without either the prior written permission of the Publishers or a licence
permitting restricted copying in Ireland issued by the Irish Copyright
Licensing Agency Ltd, The Irish Writers' Centre, 19 Parnell Square,
Dublin 1.

ISBN 978 85594 201 1 paperback

Typesetting by Mark Heslington, Scarborough, North Yorkshire
Printed and bound by CPI Group (UK) Ltd, Croydon, CR0 4YY

For Ragner

CONTENTS

Preface ix

Acknowledgements xvii

1 Wuff Wuff Wuff for de Valera! 1

2 The Flowering 9

3 Midwife to the Fairies 22

4 The Wife of Bath 31

5 The Catechism Examination 44

6 Blood and Water 52

7 A Visit to Newgrange 63

8 Night of the Fox 72

9 Holiday in the Land of Murdered Dreams 83

10 The Garden of Eden 120

11 Fufilment 128

12 Peacocks 143

Preface

Diversity is a signal feature of Éilís Ní Dhuibhne's multifaceted career. She has produced work variously as a folklorist, dramatist, short-story writer, novelist, editor, literary historian and – under the pseudonym Elizabeth O'Hara – children's author. A further dimension of her creative output is the fact that she writes in Irish and has composed both plays and fiction in that language.

This compilation serves a double purpose: it revives much of Ní Dhuibhne's significant early work and it also includes fresh examples of her artistry. It gathers together stories from her first two collections, *Blood and Water* and *Eating Women is Not Recommended*, published by Attic Press in 1988 and 1991, thus retrieving them from that banishment that often befalls the initial ventures of a writer. Framing these earlier pieces are three recent fictions: 'Wuff Wuff Wuff for de Valera!', commissioned for *Loose Horses*, an innovative community project sponsored by South Dublin County Council, which was distributed free of charge in pamphlet-form to libraries, public bodies and even hairdressers; 'Holiday in the Land of Murdered Dreams', which appeared in *Ladies' Night at Finbar's Hotel*, a collaborative collection of stories by Irish women writers, employing a common setting and scenario; and 'Peacocks', a new, previously unpublished work. This volume at once furnishes a retrospective on Ní Dhuibhne's achievement to date and tracks the development of an ever-evolving aesthetic and authorial sensibility.

Despite the many modes of writing which Ní Dhuibhne espouses, her literary endeavours centre first and foremost in the realm of the short story. Her four collections, *Blood and Water, Eating Women is Not Recommended, The Inland Ice and Other Stories* and *The Pale Gold of Alaska and Other Stories*, bear witness to the distinctiveness of her creative voice and to her willingness to experiment with this most elusive and malleable of literary forms. Taking stock of her work allows us not only to explore its dominant thematic and symbolic preoccupations but also to consider some of the peculiarities of postmodern Irish narratives.

Definitions of the short story are notoriously slippery and conflicting. The very designation seems more often than not to be a misnomer. Brevity, which might appear to be its most indispensable feature, is not necessarily a prerequisite, as the disparate lengths of the tales included here make evident. Often, paradoxically, texts that seem readily to fit into this category have little interest in conveying a story.

Commentators are divided, too, about whether the allegiances of this form of fiction are with tradition or modernity. For Walter Benjamin, it is embedded in community life and communicates moral wisdom to a cohesive audience. Conversely, Frank O'Connor views it as a quintessentially modern invention that is directed at a solitary reader and concentrates on the alienation of submerged population groups. However, Ní Dhuibhne's work reveals that for her, the short story is, in fact, precariously positioned between tradition and modernity while never fully inhabiting either sphere. Despite their propensity to depict an unembellished reality, her postmodern tales often aspire to the exemplarity of myth. They also retain one of the fundamental functions of story-telling as identified by Richard Kearney, namely, the quest for symbolic solutions to the contradictions and unanswerable questions of existence.

Ní Dhuibhne's doctoral study of the many oral and literary versions of a common European narrative, used most memorably by Geoffrey Chaucer in *The Friar's Tale*, attests to her fascination, not just with the content but also with the variegated shapes assumed by stories. In her creative production, she tends to eschew linear plots, to use teasing elisions, digressions and suspended endings and to experiment with multilayered structures. Indeed, her fictions urge us to read between the lines, to become alert to gaps and omissions and to supply the broken links between seemingly unconnected events. Many of the stories collected here hinge, for example, on unspoken realizations, as in the instance of the oblique memories in 'The Catechism Examination', which recall the cruel treatment by her teacher and peers of a young girl, considered to be slow and different.

Often, too, the would-be epiphanies in these narratives appear to be vanishing points rather than moments of revelation. The shared rapture at the perfection of the Boyne valley burial chamber in 'A

Visit to Newgrange' that forces the narrator to revise her negative views of her German boyfriend's mother seems lost in the private evanescence of inner consciousness. Likewise, the magical, nocturnal sighting of a fox in 'Night of the Fox' cannot be communicated by the protagonist to her family and becomes symbolic of the elliptical, inner darkness that separates individuals. Ní Dhuibhne's dystopian novel, *The Bray House*, in which a team of Swedish archaeologists travels to Ireland with the purpose of reconstructing its culture by carrying out a dig in a countryside devastated by nuclear meltdown, also depends on an abortive climax. The records of a lone female survivor of the disaster, brutally stolen by the ambitious leader of this mission, turn out to be worthless and the meticulously compiled anthropological findings about an Irish family in the 1980s are also consigned to oblivion. As Derek Hand observes, a postmodern concern with the disjunction between discourse and reality is at the nub of this text.

Drawing upon her academic interests, Ní Dhuibhne frequently incorporates folklore into her fiction and uses it to explore the divergences and continuities between tradition and modernity in Irish society. In 'Midwife to the Fairies', a folk tale is interpolated into a contemporary story that, in fact, transposes and retells it. The double-levelled structure makes us aware of the different modes of narration that typify the oral composition and its modern analogue. It also highlights the way in which the taboos concerning pregnancy, incest and infant death that, as Diane Purkiss illustrates, are habitually associated with fairy activity, continue to hold even in a supposedly more rational era. Moreover, Ní Dhuibhne's dexterity in transliterating the legend into the vivid demotic of a contemporary Dublin midwife reinforces the eeriness of the folk exemplar rather than dissipating its power.

A more elaborate variant on this technique of interweaving oral material with postmodern perspectives may be found in *The Inland Ice*. Here, instalments of a folk tale, 'The Search for the Lost Husband', are interspersed between the stories in the collection. Once again a fusion of horizons is achieved. Even though the segmented tale replicates the ritualistic repetitions and the starkly concise style of oral narration, the ending, in which the woman finally rejects the tyranny of her shape-changing husband, mirrors the struggle of many of Ní Dhuibhne's fictional heroines to come to grips with the problem of desire and to achieve independence.

The importance of voice and of conflicting forms of speech in the exploration of the inner and outer worlds of her characters seems to owe much to the author's understanding of how orality structures our psychic economies. The complex ironies, for example, of the conclusion of 'Wuff Wuff Wuff for de Valera!' depend on the juxtaposition of a children's rhyme, a forceful remnent from oral culture, and the contorted dishonesty of the internal monologue of the protagonist. In addition, the frequent use of first-person narratives, which is a particular hallmark of Ní Dhuibhne's early stories, allows for a mingling of postmodern dissonance with the immediacy of direct address. The disjointed reminiscences of the narrator in 'The Catechism Examination' are all the more searing because their meaning seems invisible to the speaker herself. Likewise, the absurdity of the pursuits of the psychopathic canine-murderer in 'Fulfilment' is further underscored because her narrative insists on its normality.

A by-product of the accelerated changes in Irish society in the 1990s, chiefly as a result of the short-lived economic phenomenon of the Celtic Tiger, has been the disavowal of the past on many fronts. Such historical amnesia is foreign to the work of Ní Dhuibhne. More than any other contemporary Irish writer, she explores the gaps between decades of the late twentieth century that appear to be contiguous and shows how the tensions between competing timeframes and value systems are at the basis of the moral and emotional dilemmas of her characters. The uncanny familiarity and oddity of the past are central preoccupations of many of her stories.

In 'The Flowering', the central protagonist, Lennie, searches for vital clues in her family history that might enable her to make sense of herself. She conjures up the tragic story of Sally Rua, a female forebear, who descends into madness because she is denied the chance to pursue the lace-making craft at which she excels. This absorbing biography is, however, unexpectedly deconstructed in the final paragraphs. The past, as a consequence, is shown to be both a repository for alternative selves and the source of figments and inventions. It can be neither dismissed nor easily harnessed to cancel out the fragmentation that seems the lot of the postmodern heroine.

The estranging but also clarifying effect of anterior selves is a key facet of the exploration of the past in 'Blood and Water'. Split between childhood and adult perspectives, the narrator in this story describes her mingled feelings of delight and disgust during family holidays spent in Donegal. Her ambivalence centres especially on the figure of her aunt whose oddities and simple-mindedness arouse an abhorrence that eventually cedes to pity. A blob of butter smeared on the wall of her relative's farmhouse, which she later learns is a folk ritual to ensure good fortune, becomes emblematic of her distress at the polluting otherness of this rural world.

Her violent reaction to her aunt stems, it emerges, from the family likeness they share. Hence her contradictory feelings of fascinated recoil are akin to the fractured responses elicited by a *Doppelgänger* who is at once a surrogate and an anti-self. In short, the identity of the protagonist of this story is depicted as revolving around ethnic, spatial and historical divisions that refuse either to disappear or to assume coherence. Retrospection rarely permits the consolation of revisionism for Ní Dhuibhne's heroines. Rather, the past, their previous selves and the other Irelands that they have inhabited continue to haunt and configure their emotional and intellectual landscapes.

Éilís Ní Dhuibhne's recent *Bildungsroman, The Dancers Dancing*, skilfully recasts several incidents from 'Blood and Water' and fundamentally alters their trajectory. The experiences of three Dublin girls attending Irish college in the Donegal Gaeltacht are described as an essential rite of passage from adolescence to adulthood. With its vivid depiction of the details of Irish life in the 1970s, the novel is at once an ethnographic fiction and a celebratory tale of sexual and emotional awakening. As the title indicates, mobility and physical pleasure are key components of this holiday interlude. The teenage dancers at the exuberant céilís, overseen by the benign presence of Headmaster Joe, joyfully submerge themselves in the immediacy of experience. In keeping with the giddy energies of this narrative, the dark spectre of the grotesque aunt is banished when it transpires that she is a personage of note due to her stock of local folklore.

Despite this happy resolution, the novel, like the story out of which it developed, registers the divisions between temporalities. Fragments from the shadowy history of a local woman, who was hanged for drowning her new-born baby, cut across the plot, while a final chapter that fast-forwards to the present and the remove of adulthood reveals how modernity, loss and the bittersweet intensity of memory inflect the subtly altered inner world of the central heroine.

Above all else, Ní Dhuibhne's fictions reconnoitre the problematic aspects of contemporary female experience. The tensions between women's internal perspectives on themselves and the conflicting social roles they are expected to fulfil as mothers, daughters and lovers are recurrent themes of her work. In particular, her protagonists have to grapple with what Efrat Tseëlon terms the 'masque of femininity', that is, negative definitions of female selfhood as non-identity and artifice. The conflicted nature of female subjectivity is thematized in 'Peacocks'. Here, the anorexia of the protagonist's daughter repeats her erstwhile obsession with dieting as a young woman. An unsettling re-encounter with a Spanish lover brings home to her that her appearance in middle age equally depends on an artificially cultivated self-projection. In fact, she realizes that she now imitates the corpulent sexuality of the Welsh chambermaid whose boyfriend she had stolen. The troubling denouement intimates that the unresolved hostilities between mother and daughter stem from the amorality of erotic love and the dangerous instability of female identity in a male-dominated society.

Marina Warner has pointed out that postmodern anxieties about the changing nature of femininity have led to a resurgence of myths featuring the metamorphoses of the monstrous female. Several of Ní Dhuibhne's stories in this collection pick up on and playfully engage with such plots. The stout self-justifications of the dog-murdering anti-heroine of 'Fulfilment' comically override any misogynist imputations of perversity. In contrast, the bizarre kleptomania of the protagonist in 'The Garden of Eden' is revealed to have tragic roots and to be instigated by her unhappy marriage and repressed grief for her dead son.

Increasingly, in her recent fictions, Ní Dhuibhne's heroines, beset by the impropriety and irrational nature of their desires, are painted as transients and travellers between worlds. Intercultural settings allegorize the wavering identities of her female dramatis personae. Her later plots routinely make use of other geographical locations, such as Greenland, Sweden, France, Denmark and America, and encourage a bifurcated, comparativist view of Irish society. In 'Hot Earth', a story included in *The Inland Ice*, the vista of the funerary sculptures of reclining couples in the Etruscan museum in Volterra crystallizes the realization of a middle-aged Dublin tourist that she has become entrapped in her marriage and a pointless love affair. The finely etched love of an Irish emigrant woman from Donegal for a Black Foot Indian in 'The Pale Gold of Alaska' becomes symbolic of the illicit but also possibly liberating nature of female desire.

The vantage point of an adult life spent in Holland permits Detta in 'Holiday in the Land of Murdered Dreams', to revisit her past existence in Dublin and to take stock of the sexual and emotional compromises that she has made. Her willing abandonment of her identity during her first, fateful love affair, which ended in unwanted pregnancy, highlights not only the self-destructive aspects of passivity and Irish female socialization but also the positive potential of the readiness to embrace difference.

Alice Munro has described the process of reading a short story as akin to wandering back and forth inside a house, discovering how the corridors and rooms interconnect and appreciating how the views from the windows change our perspective on the terrain outside. In a similar fashion, the complex layers and sudden veerings of Éilís Ní Dhuibhne's economic, suggestive and open-ended tales give solidity to a shared world of meaning but also invite us freely to navigate the imaginary spaces that she constructs. In particular, her fiction makes us aware of the fluctuating and often self-deceptive nature of our internal dialogues and of the need to remain attuned both to the past and to the former selves and attitudes that we thought we had shed.

Anne Fogarty

REFERENCES:

Walter Benjamin, 'The Storyteller: Reflections on the Works of Nikolai Leskov', in Hannah Arendt (ed.), *Illuminations* (London: Fontana, 1973)

Derek Hand, 'Being Ordinary – Ireland from Elsewhere: A Reading of Éilís Ní Dhuibhne's *The Bray House*', *Irish University Review*, *Special Issue: Irish Contemporary Fiction*, Anthony Roche (ed.), vol. 30, Spring/Summer 2000, 103–116

Richard Kearney, *On Stories* (London: Routledge, 2002)

Alice Munro, 'What Is Real?', in John Metcalf (ed.), *Making It New: Contemporary Canadian Short Stories* (Toronto: Methuen, 1982)

Éilís Ní Dhuibhne, *Blood and Water* (Dublin: Attic Press, 1988)

—— *The Bray House* (Dublin: Attic Press, 1990)

—— *Eating Women Is Not Recommended* (Dublin: Attic Press, 1991)

—— *The Inland Ice and Other Stories* (Belfast: The Blackstaff Press, 1997)

—— *The Dancers Dancing* (Belfast: The Blackstaff Press, 1999)

—— *The Pale Gold of Alaska and Other Stories* (Belfast: The Blackstaff Press, 2000)

—— 'Fer in the North Contree: "With His Whole Heart" Revisited', in Séamas Ó'Catháin (ed.) *Northern Lights: Following Folklore in Northwestern Europe. Essays in Honour of Bo Almqvist* (Dublin: Unversity College Dublin Press, 2001)

Frank O'Connor, *The Lonely Voice: A Study of the Short Story* (London: Macmillan, 1963)

Diane Purkiss, *Troublesome Things: A History of Fairies and Fairy Stories* (London: Penguin, 2001).

Efrat Tseëlon. *The Masque of Femininity : The Presentation of Woman in Everyday Life* (London: Sage, 1995)

Marina Warner, *Managing Monsters: Six Myths of Our Time. The 1994 Reith Lectures* (London: Vintage, 1994)

Acknowledgements

Most of these stories were originally published in book form in *Blood and Water* (Attic Press 1989) and *Eating Women is Not Recommended* (Attic Press 1991).

'The Hotel of Murdered Dreams' was originally published under the title "The Master Key" in *Ladies' Night at Finbar's Hotel*, ed. Dermot Bolger, New Island Books/Picador 1999; 'Wuff Wuff Wuff for De Valera' in *Wild Horses*, ed. Lia Mills, South Dublin County Council, 2001; 'The Flowering' and 'Midwife to the Fairies' in *The Blackstaff Book of Short Stories*, 1988; 'The Catechism Examination' and 'Blood and Water' in New Irish Writing, *The Irish Press*; 'A Visit to Newgrange' and 'The Garden of Eden' in *The Irish Times*; 'Fulfilment' in *Panurge*.

1

WUFF WUFF WUFF
FOR DE VALERA!

My sister and I were going down to Lanzarote, on a cheapie little week away from the February rain. My real holidays will be later with Conor and Emma who for a wonder has consented to come with us. We're doing a safari in Zimbabwe and Emma loves animals and ecology and all that crap. That'll be it for this year, actually, because we're going to buy a cottage somewhere in Umbria, which we love, and that means I'll be up and down, up and down, looking at places and probably buying one and fitting it out in the end. Conor is much busier than I am, and less flexible. When we've got the place he'll get long weekends there and so on but I know, in spite of his best intentions, he won't be getting there much until it's all set up. I'm very flexible.

The Lanzarote thing was to be my treat but Pauline wouldn't hear of it, so we were going Dutch. It took the fun out of it. She always seems to be so hard-pressed for cash, being something in the corporation, one of those 1950s sort of jobs nobody has nowadays that is steady and offers you a pension when you retire, but no fun in the meantime. And I've never understood why she stayed in it for so long, but I suppose that's history. When she was at an age to move on there was nowhere to move on to. By the time the change in the economy came Pauline was too old to take advantage of it. You get into a rut, I guess. I didn't but everything was different for me – marriage can be a safety net, let's face facts.

Pauline has hardly been abroad on holidays at all. That's more to do with Sebastian and his needs than money, I mean anyone can afford Ryanair, and there's all those Superquinn breaks and so on, so money is hardly an excuse, isn't it true? But there you are, she is excited at the airport, in a way I haven't been since I was about twenty – I was over twenty when I went abroad, first, that's how it was back then.

'Where do we go now?' she asked, when we'd checked in, and she couldn't hide the mixture of nervousness and delight in her voice. It almost made me cry, to think that she didn't know the way to the departure gates, a walk I make about forty times a year, at least. 'I'll lead the way!' I say brightly, pushing out the trolley. At least both our bags look identical, although I know Pauline bought hers in Dunnes Stores and mine is a tougher, more enduring brand, which it has to be, it gets such a lot of wear and tear. She is looking good, too, better than most people in the airport. A lot of Irish people don't know how to dress for travelling; I make a habit of watching them in the departure lounge, to see who manages to look appropriate, and smart. Hardly anyone. Research has shown me that the Germans do it best. You should wear, for business, a black suit, white blouse, and perfect accessories. For holidays that looks stupid. What you need is crease-proof cotton jeans, leather walking shoes, a crisp white t-shirt or shirt, and a casual jacket, suede or leather. Beige or navy are appropriate colours. Pauline doesn't have a leather jacket, of course, but her waterproof is a good substitute, and otherwise she looks perfect, as far as the clothes are concerned, I mean. Her face is a wreck. Too much worry. And she's let her figure go. It is my honest opinion that if she had her teeth fixed up, or even whitened, and lost about two stone, she'd be doing a lot better in that job of hers. But there you go. If she won't let me give her a week on the Canaries she's not going to accept a voucher for the orthodontist, and weight loss is a question of willpower.

She used to be better-looking than me, and her willpower was stronger.

We're twins, but she was the first born. We lived in Crumlin in a corporation house. The street was called Mozart Road, a name that sounds nice, but most people on the road wouldn't have known Mozart from Elvis Presley. As for hearing his music – well, we didn't even own a record player, and it was pre-Elvira-Madigan-while-you-pick-the-cornflakes days.

But outside, 'out playing' was another story. A wonderland. A symphony of children's sounds: laughs, screams, cries, whoops. Hula hoops whirring, skipping ropes smacking the tarmac, balls walloping walls. We sang all day long, skipping rhymes, ball rhymes, counting out rhymes. 'In and out goes Mary Bluebell'. 'Plainy packet a rinso'. 'Vote vote vote for de Valera', in goes Pauline and the door I O, Pauline is the one that can have a bit of fun and we don't want Bernie any more I O.'

(I heard children singing that rhyme a few years ago, on a road not far from my neighbourhood. 'Wuff Wuff Wuff for de Valera!' they sang. They obviously didn't know who de Valera was, but the rhyme endured, to my astonishment. I didn't think kids could even skip any more, let alone sing those songs. They sort of seem to belong to another era, the Mozart Road era.)

Pauline was always the one who stage managed the games – decided what we'd play, who was 'on it', who got to pick the sides. At home she was domineering too, insofar as she could be – not very far. Children were encouraged to be meek, in those days. Once Pauline went on hunger strike, made me go on it too, because our mother wouldn't take us to the park. We struck for two days. Then our mother went into labour with our brother Frankie. Our daddy slapped us for being bold – he somehow believed that we had induced the labour; obstetrics wasn't his forte. Pauline sulked but ended the strike, since Mammy was in hospital anyway and Daddy never brought us anywhere, not even to the shops.

But Pauline never lost it. In 1971 when we were seventeen and doing the Leaving she decided we were going to university, which was the equivalent of staging the October Revolution in Mozart Road; nobody on Mozart Road had ever gone to university. In fact we were the first bunch even to go to secondary school, free education having been introduced in the nick of time, just as we finished primary. Somehow that caught on very fast – almost everyone went. But nobody else went to college. We had one of those quaint working-class childhoods Irish writers are always going on about: scruffy corner shops, luke-warm baths once a week, disasterous clothes. Inside, in the house, life was drab. We went to Trinity; she loved *Brideshead Revisited* and Trinity was the closest she could get to Oxbridge. Her imagination was even wilder than her ambition. Though it had its limits: College Green.

'We're going everywhere!' she said. 'We're not spending our lives stuck in an insurance office.' Insurance was a favourite career for the brightest sparks from Mozart Road, the Donogh O Malley first fruits, that and the civil service. 'For us it's going to be different. Rome Parish Trieste!' She read Joyce, too.

I believed it. Going to Trinity was a leap so major that after that everything was going to seem like baby steps. And in a way for me it has all worked out. I never travelled in the sense we had intended to – you see I met Conor in second year and we got married three years later and that sort of ended the wanderlust bit, since he decided to make his career here (he was an accountant but he moved into management in the late seventies). But I've seen practically everything I want to see, on holidays, and when Emma gets her degree I'll go away for longer stretches.

What happened to Pauline?

She was doing fine. We did Arts, needless to say. She wanted to take on medicine but even she baulked at the idea of a six-year course, and anyway she wasn't great at maths and science. So we did English and Spanish – Spanish being the language they always taught in poor schools, while the fee-paying ones did French, I never knew why exactly, unless it is that a lot of poor people all over the world speak Spanish. Trinity made a big impression on us but we made none at all on Trinity; we melted into the granite walls, silent shadows who did our work, sat in the library till closing time (studying at home was almost impossible) and didn't participate at all in social life. At the end of first year we got good marks but nothing spectacular enough to attract anyone's attention, and although Pauline loved to talk about books she didn't, in tutorials, because the tutors had difficulty understanding her Crumlin accent and weren't very tactful about keeping their problem to themselves. After one of them asked her to repeat a Hiberno-English phrase she'd used in class – she had said 'I'm after saying that already' – she kept quiet. Hiberno-English! Everyone looked at her as if she had strayed off an Abbey set.

In second year she got pregnant.

That's what happened to her. That's why she sort of didn't make it. I think so.

'I want to have an abortion,' she said, when she told me. Girls had them, Trinity girls. But they were always at a distance which made them impossible to access. Sometimes I wonder if they were mythical creatures. They were certainly as elusive as dryads or mermaids. You heard about them, but you never actually saw one, much less talked to one or asked them for advice.

There was a family-planning clinic in Dublin then, to which people went for contraceptives, which were still illegal, even for married people, but if you were brave and in the know you could go to one of these clinics and get the pill or condoms. So we sneaked off to it, looking over our shoulders in case anyone we knew would spot us. It was located in a quiet back street, in a basement. We slunk down damp area steps into the centre, which turned out to be very nice: painted pale green and pink and with a print of Van Gogh's *Sunflowers* on the wall. That counted as vaguely with it, avant-garde, to us anyway. If I'd had a flat, which I never did, it would have looked like this, I thought, as I sat and waited. I always watched and picked up tips on style, even then. Style is, I suppose, my main interest in life, although I have never really admitted that to anyone. I like things to look nice. I really do.

The staff all seemed to be English, or to have accents that sounded English – a bit like Trinity, so we weren't as fazed as we might have been. They were very slow to give us information about abortion – they tried everything else: to persuade Pauline to get married, to consider adoption, to keep the baby. All impossible for her – the boy wouldn't marry her and she didn't want to anyway. If she went through with the pregnancy she'd miss her exams and then wouldn't get her grant next year. And keeping the baby . . . where would she keep it? On what? Nobody did that. Nobody would talk to you, if you did. You'd be a leper.

In the end, they gave her a London telephone number.

Even phoning London was a huge undertaking for us. We didn't have a phone at home and couldn't have used it if we had. We went to the GPO into one of those brown boxes with the swing doors they have, or had, there. We had piles of fivepenny pieces. We had to go through an operator and we were terrified that she would find out who we were phoning: maybe someone would answer 'Central Abortion Clinic' or something. But that didn't happen. They were discreet on the phone. They told us, discreetly, that the cost of the procedure plus a night in the clinic would be £300.

5

Three hundred pounds. And travel on top of that. It might as well have been three million pounds. Our fees for the year were about a hundred pounds. Our maintenance grant for the year was £200, and our mother got that. We had no money. We had no friends with money. We'd never gone to England, never booked a ticket on the ferry, never stayed in a hotel or a B. and B. It was all too much for us.

She missed the exams. One of the Catholic agencies for unmarried mothers organized everything for her – home, hospital, adoption. But it misfired. When she had the baby, at one of those homes, it was mentally retarded, so the couple who had it earmarked backed off and nobody else wanted it. Pauline could have left the baby – Sebastian – in the home but she wouldn't. She hated institutions.

'I wouldn't have let them adopt him either, after I'd had it' she said (she probably believed this). 'It was like he was . . . part of me. Giving him up for adoption would have been like cutting off my arm and giving it to someone who hadn't got an arm of their own, sort of. Do you know what I mean? It would've been worse than that.'

I've had Emma, and Matthew, who's at Cambridge now. I know what she means. You just adore them when they're born (I mean I still do of course, but there's that overwhelming biological bond, when they're tiny. I used to weep leaving them in the crèche to go to work, which I still did when they were small, before Conor branched out on his own. I missed them much more than they missed me! Of course they loved the crèche; sometimes they cried when I came to pick them up! They're as tough as old boots really).

She used to leave the baby in with a woman in Iveagh Gardens while she was at work, and I babysat a good bit during the first couple of years. Later Sebastian went to a day-care centre which kept him for most of the day. He's old now, thirty, but he still lives with her. She's everything to him. And vice versa. I know her main worry is what will happen to him if anything goes wrong. She did get a degree in the end – she did one of those night modules in UCD, in philosophy and Greek and Roman Civilization. She owns her own house, even – she bought a privatized corporation house in Kimmage ages ago, so she's fine from that point of view. I don't know why she's never got a lot of promotion, maybe she's a bit too forthright about her atheism, her dislike of the Catholic Church, that sort of thing. And she probably should have done something on marketing or business studies instead of philosophy. I mean she works in the sewerage section, I can't imagine philosophy is very relevant. Plus she's overweight and sloppy looking and she goes on and on about being a single parent. Even today it's wiser to be discreet about that but Pauline has made a huge issue out of it, being Pauline.

'This is the life!' she says. We're sitting beside the little pool outside our apartment, drinking red wine. She drinks too much wine, maybe that's the root of her weight problem.

'Yes isn't it?' I say.

'Do you ever wish you'd had the money, for that abortion?' I ask. It was our fourth day out, and it had gone well. It had been great actually. I'd got quite a nice tan and had drunk I'd say a bottle of wine already, you know how you can if you get started. I'll pay for that next week. But the starvation diet is the easiest of all, once you get used to it, and at least it works. We'd never discussed the abortion thing, not for about thirty years.

She didn't really answer. She just smiled and then she started to sing. 'Wuff wuff wuff for de Valera!

> In comes Bernie at the door I O.
> Bernie is the one that can have a bit of fun
> and we don't want Pauline any more I O.'

I was amazed. I didn't know anybody else knew that version, apart from me. But there you are. You think something is your own secret and then you find out it's common knowledge. Always the way, isn't it?

I'd already met Conor when Pauline got pregnant; I'd met him at the Elizabethan garden party. His father was an accountant, like him, and he seemed to me to be steeped in money, like most of the other students. I sort of thought I could have asked him for the £300. But

I'd just been with him for about a month; he didn't even know I had a sister. How do you ask the boy you've just started going with for £300 so your sister can have an abortion? Conor was a lapsed Catholic, like us, but I didn't know how far he'd lapsed, you know? (Not too far, was the answer – as soon as we had Matt we all went right back to weekly Mass, although naturally we draw the line at confession, the guff about contraception, and so on. But it's better for the kids to be Catholic and of course it's essential for your career, something people like Pauline never got into their thick heads.) I digress. Anyway, there was all that. Plus, more important, it was a big deal for Conor, dating a girl from Crumlin – he lived in Palmerston Park, where we live now, in the same house. We got it when his mother finally kicked the bucket last year. It was a miracle, it was going to take a miracle, to get Conor to marry me at all. On top of Mozart Road, my Hiberno-English, my lack of pedigree, a sister who was having an abortion would be just too much.

So I didn't risk it.

2

THE FLOWERING

Lennie has a dream, a commonplace, even a vulgar dream, and one which she knows is unlikely to be realized. She wants to discover her roots. Not just names and dates from parish registers or census returns. Those she can find easily enough, insofar as they exist at all. What she desires is a real, a true discovery. An unearthing of homes, a peeling off of clothes and trappings, a revelation of minds, an excavation of hearts.

Why she wants this she does not know, or knows only very vaguely. It is partly a general curiosity about the past of her family, and more particularly a thirst for self-knowledge. Why does she look this way? Like some things and not others? Why does she do some things and not others? If she knew which traits she has inherited from whom, which are independent qualities, surely she would be a better judge of what she is herself, or of what she can become?

When she begins to ask these questions she becomes excited, initially, then dizzy. The litany of queries is self-propagating. It enjoys a frenzied beanstalk growth but reaches no satisfactory conclusions. And the more it expands, the more convinced is Lennie that the answers are important. The promise, or rather the hope, of solutions, glows like a lantern in the bottle-green, the black cave of her mind, where Plato's shadows sometimes hover but more often do not make an appearance at all. Drunk on questions, she begins to believe that there is one answer, a true all-encompassing resolution which will flood that dim region with brilliant light for once and for all, illuminating all personal conundrums.

Of course when Lennie sobers up she knows that such an answer is impossible. The only thing she has learnt about the truth – she believes in its existence; that is her one act of faith – is that it is many-faceted. This is as true of the past as it is of the present and the future. Knowledge of ancestors would not tell her all she needed to know, in order to see herself, or anything, clearly. But it would provide a clue or two.

Clues. There are a few. Place, in particular, looks promising. The same location for hundreds of years, if popular belief holds any veracity – the documents suggest that it does. Wavesend. Low hills swoop, black and purple and bright moss green, into darker green fields. Yellow ragweed and cow parsley decorate them. Royal red fuchsia, pink dog-roses, meadowsweet and foxgloves flounce in the ditches that line the muddy lane leading down to the shore. Leonine haunches of sand roll into the golden water of the lough. Golden lough, turquoise lough, indigo lough, jade lough. Black lough, lake of shadows. The shadows are the clouds, always scudding across the high opalescent sky. The terns, the oystercatchers, the gulls swoop into those and their own shadows after shadows of herrings, shoals of shadowy mackerel. Shadows on the other side of the shadowy looking-glass of the water.

The house of stone, two storeys high, with undersized door and narrow windows squinting in the grey walls. Crosseyed, shortsighted house, peering at the byre across the 'street'. A cobbled path brings people limping there to milk the cows, or if they are women, and usually they are, since cows are women's work, go to the toilet. The milk bounces into wooden buckets, the other flows through a neat square hole into the green stinking pond. The midden. A ridiculous word which always made Lennie laugh. Piddle, middie, midden. Riddle.

Inside, dark is relieved by bright painted furniture. The blue dresser displaying floral tea-bowls, willow patterned platters, huge jugs with red roses floating in pinky-blue clouds on their bellies – the jugs came free, full of raspberry jam; that's why there are so many of them. A special dock, known as an American clock, with a brass pendulum and a sunray crown. Red bins for corn and layers' mash.

The stuff of folk museums. Lennie gets it from textbooks (*Irish Folk Ways*) and from exhibition catalogues, as well as from her own memory. The exhibited model and the actual house overlap so much that it is difficult to distinguish one from the other now. In her own lifetime – she is in her thirties, neither young nor old – real life has entered the museum and turned into history. A real language has crept into the sound archives of linguistic departments and folklore institutions, and it has faded away from people's tongues. In one or two generations. In *her* generation. It has been a time of endings. Of deaths, great and small. But this she finds interesting rather than painful. She was, after all, an observer of life in Wavesend, someone who had already moved on to other ways of living and speaking before she came to know it and its ways, before she grew to realize their importance. She was never really part of the Wavesend way of life and so she was not confounded or offended by its embalming and burial while some of its organs still lived on, weakly flapping like the limbs of an executed man. Saddened she was, but not bewildered.

Other clues to her past are folk-museum stuff, school history stuff, too. The Famine. Seaweed and barnacles and herrings for dinner. A bowl of yellow meal given to a tinker caused her immediate death. Ate the meal and dropped dead on the hot kitchen floor, Glory be to God; she hadn't eaten in a month, the stomach couldn't take it. Lennie's ancestors had yellow meal, and seaweed, and barnacles, so they survived, or some of them survived. What does that tell her about them? The litany goes on. Oh Mother Most Astute! Oh Mother Most Hungry! Oh Mother Most Merciful! Oh Mother Most Cruel! Give us our gruel! The Lennies turned, became Protestant, and later turned back again. Some of them went to America and later came back again.

Wolfe Tone passed by the house on his way to France. Drugged. Red Hugh passed by the house on his way to Dublin. Drunk. Lennie's great-great-great-grandmother saw the ship and waved.

The Great War. Artillery practice on the shores of the Lough. The sound of cannon reverberates across the night-still waters. Boom. Men stir in their heavy sleep. Boom. An infant shrieks. In the fragile shelter of daylight soldiers visit the house to buy milk and eggs. So, were they friendly? Did they chat? Did someone fall in love with one of them? They gave Lennie's father a ride in a car. His first car ride. That's the sum total of it. It must have been exciting, Daddy! It was. It was.

11

A personal experience tale: when Daddy was seven he fell off a bike, a man's big bike that he had been riding with his legs under instead of over the crossbar. Ten months in a Derry hospital followed the experience. The wound on his leg would not heal. Home, with the abscess, to live or die. Philoctetes. Folk belief: the miracle cure. A holy stone from the holy well, the well of St Patrick, was taken by his grandmother. You shouldn't take stones from shrines or ancient sites of worship, from open air museums, but people did not know that then. She took it home without a by your leave and placed it on the wounded spot, and the next day she returned it to its ancient site. The wound healed. He always limped but he was healed by whatever was in that stone.

And what was it like, in hospital for ten months all alone? Not a single visit for the little nine-year-old boy. Not a single visit. He forgets. He doesn't remember it at all. Perhaps he cannot afford to remember.

It's enough to drive you crazy. Archaeology, history, folklore. Linguistics, genealogy. They tell you about society, not about individuals. It takes literature to do that. And since the Lennies couldn't write until Lennie's grandparents went to school, and not very much after that, there isn't any literature. Not now anyway. The oral tradition. What oral tradition? It went away, with their language, when the schools started. Slowly they are becoming articulate in the new language. Slowly they are finding a new tradition. They are inventing a new tradition. Transform, adopt, or disappear.

But look, there she is, hunkered over the black stool in the bottle-green dimness of that cavernous byre, her long hair cloaking her visage and her long, adroit hands squeezing the hot teats. There she is! Sally Rua. Lennie's great-aunt. A tall girl, with adder-green eyes and a mole on her chin and two moles on the sole of her right foot. Gentle on the whole, sometimes acerbic and brusque. People who dislike her – women, mostly, because she is the sort of reserved woman many men unaccountably gravitate towards – say she is a snake. When her hair is wound up behind her long white neck, the simile is accurate enough, although boys who love her compare her, more conventionally, to a swan.

She lived in that house in Wavesend, slept in the bedroom with the window that has to be propped open with a stick and the green wardrobe with cream borders that her own father made for her. In the mornings she went to school in the low white cottage beside the church. The rest of the day she was engaged in all the busy activities of the home. Baking and boiling, feeding and milking. Teasing and carding and spinning and weaving and knitting and sewing and washing and ironing. And making sups of tea for the endless stream of callers. Rakers, they called them, those who shortened the day and the night and stole the working time. A hundred thousand welcomes to you. Just wait till I finish this skein.

When Sally Rua was thirteen a lady from Monaghan, a Miss Burns, came to Wavesend to open a lacemaking school there. The Congested Districts Board had sent her, and her brief was to teach twelve likely girls a craft which would help them supplement their family income. The craft was crochet. The people of Wavesend, and Miss Burns too, called it 'flowering'. Twelve girls, including Sally Rua, assembled in a room in the real teacher's house, which had been kindly lent to Miss Burns. There she began to teach them the rudiments of her craft.

Miss Burns was thirty-six, pretty and mellow, not mad and volatile like Miss Gallagher, the real teacher who was lending them her room. She wore snow-white, high-necked blouses with a dark-blue or a dark-green skirt, and her hair was fair. Leafy brown, fastened to the nape of her neck in a loose bun. Her face was imperfect. There were hairs on her upper lip, quite a little moustache, and Sally Rua thought that this softened her, made her gentler and more pleasant than she might otherwise have been; more cheerful, more enthusiastic about her work of teaching country girls to crochet.

The atmosphere in the chilly room where they worked around a big table was light-hearted. An atmosphere of well-aired orderliness, appropriate to the task in hand. It had less to do with the embroidery, or even with Miss Burns, Sally Rua thought, than with the fact that boys were absent. This resulted in a loss of excitement, of the difficult but not unappealing tension which tautened the air in the ordinary classroom, so that no matter what anyone was doing they were vigilant, aware that extraordinary things were going on all the time under the apparently predictable surface of lessons and timetables. Here in the single sex embroidery class there was none of that; only peace and concentration.

The first thing they learned to crochet was a rose. Sally Rua had sewed the clinching stitch and severed her thread by the end of the first day, although most of the other girls spent a week completing the project. By then, Sally Rua could do daisies, grapes, and shamrocks, and had produced a border of the latter for a linen handkerchief. She worked on her embroidery at home as well as at the school, gaining extra light at night by placing a glass jug of water beside the candle, a trick Miss Burns taught them on the first day. (She had also told them that a good place to store the embroidery, to keep it clean, was under the pillow, unless they happened to have a box or a tin. Nobody had.) 'You've already learnt all I'm supposed to teach you!' said Miss Burns at the end of the week, smiling kindly but with some nervousness at Sally Rua. She had encountered star pupils before and was not afraid of them, but there was always the problem of what to teach next, and the suspicion that they already knew more than the teacher. 'You could stop coming here, if you liked. You can already earn money.'

Sally Rua did not want to stop coming. Her primary education was over now – the flowering was by way of finishing school. The prospect of spending her mornings sitting outside the house at home, working alone in the early light, and being called upon to do a thousand and one chores, was not immediately appealing. She'd be doing it soon enough anyhow.

'Maybe you can show me how to do that?' She pointed at a large piece of work lying on the table. It was a half-finished picture of a swan on a lake. Miss Burns had drawn the picture on a piece of paper and pinned some net to it. Now she was outlining the shape of the swan with stitches.

'That?' Miss Burns was confused. 'You won't be able to do that. I mean, you won't be able to get rid of it. The Board wants handkerchiefs, not this type of thing.'

'What is it called?'

It was Carrickmacross lace: appliqué. Miss Burns, who came from Carrickmacross, or near it, was doing a piece for her sister who was getting married in a few months' time. The 'picture' was to form the centrepiece of a white tablecloth for the sister's new dining-room.

Sally Rua offered to finish it for her, if she showed her what to do, and after some deliberation Miss Burns agreed to this, although it was not strictly ethical. However, Sally Rua continued to do her roses and daisies, and was earning twice as much money as any of the other girls already, so the aims of the Congested District Board were not being thwarted. And Miss Burns was finding the swan tedious.

It was slow work. Sally Rua spent over a week completing the stitching, which looked anaemic and almost invisible against the background of its own colour. Then the paper behind was cut away. And the scene came miraculously to life, etched into the transparent net with a strong white line.

'It's like a picture drawn on ice,' said Sally Rua. In the centre of the hills behind Wavesend, which were called, romantically but graphically, the Hills of the Swan, was a lake, the habitat of several of those birds. Every winter it froze over: the climate was colder in those days than it is now in Donegal. The children of Wavesend climbed the hills in order to slide, and Sally Rua had often done that herself, and had seen crude pictures drawn on the glossy surface with the blades of skates. Once, she had seen something else: a swan, or rather the skeleton of a swan, frozen to the ice, picked clean by stronger, luckier birds.

Miss Burns gave Sally Rua cloth and net to do a second piece of appliqué. She allowed her to make her own pattern, and suggested a few herself: doves, stags, flowers. Sally Rua drew some foxgloves and fuchsias, in a surround of roses, and this was approved of. It was a complicated pattern to work but she managed to do it. Miss Burns said she would send the piece to a shop in Dublin that sold such embroidery, and gave Sally Rua more material. This time, she did a hare leaping over a low stone wall. There were clouds in the background and a gibbous moon.

'It's beautiful,' said Miss Burns. 'But I'm not sure . . . it's very unusual.'

'I've often seen that,' said Sally Rua, who had never seen a stag or a dove and had already done the flowers. 'It's not unusual.'

'Well,' said Miss Burns, 'we'll see.

The shop in Dublin wrote back three weeks later, Miss Burns's last week, and said that they liked the appliqué and were going to send it to New York, where it would be on exhibition at the Irish Stand at a great fair, the World's Fair. They enclosed a guinea for Sally Rua, from which Miss Burns deducted 9p. for the material she had supplied.

'You should buy some more net and cambric with some of that money,' Miss Burns advised. 'The address of the shop in Dublin is Brown Thomas and Company, Grafton Street. Do another piece of that Carrickmacross and send it to them. You are doing it better than they can do it in the convents.' And she added, because she was a kind and an honest woman: 'You can flower better than me now, too, you know. You should be the teacher, not I.'

Sally Rua, who had known she was better than Miss Burns on her first day's flowering, took her teacher's advice. She walked seven miles to Rathmullan, the nearest town to Wavesend, and bought some yards of net and cambric. She created appliquéd pictures of seagulls swimming on the waves of the lough, of an oystercatcher flying through the great arch at Portsalon, and of the tub-shaped coracles from which her father and brothers fished. Each of these pictures was despatched to Brown Thomas's, and for each of them she was paid ten and sixpence, half of what had been paid for the first, and, it seemed to her, inferior piece. She heard no more about that or about how it had been received at the World's Fair.

The time required to do the appliqué work was extensive, and in fact it did not pay as well as the ordinary flowering. Sally Rua continued to do a lot of that, although she did not particularly enjoy it. However, she could turn out a few dozen roses or daisies a week, and that was what the merchant who called to the school in Wavesend every Friday afternoon wanted. For every flower she received 4p. The money formed a useful contribution to the family economy, and so the aim of the Congested District Board was fulfilled, and Sally Rua's life settled into a pattern which she found rewarding: flowering and housework by day, appliquéing (and some other forms of entertainment) by night. She was happier than she had ever been before.

It did not last. By September, Miss Burns had left Wavesend and the lacemaking school had stopped. In March of the following year, six pictures later, Sally Rua's father and two brothers were drowned while fishing on the lough during a storm. When the wake and funeral were over and the first grieving past, the practical implications of the disaster were outlined to Sally Rua by her mother. She could no longer afford to live on the farm at Wavesend unless her daughters went out and earned a living (the only son, Denis, was married). The flowering would not be enough. Sally Rua would have to get a real job, one that would support her fully and leave some money over for her mother.

She went to work as a maid in a house in Rathmullan, the house of the doctor, Doctor Lynch. She was the lucky one; Mary Kate and Janey, her sisters, had to go to the Lagan to work as hired girls for farmers. Sally Rua's polish, and her reputation as a skilled needle-worker, ensured that she had the better fate.

The house in Rathmullan was a square stone block on a low slope overlooking the roofs of the town. It was called 'The Rookery', because it was close to a wood where thousands of crows nested. Sally Rua's room was in the attic, of course, at the back of the house, above the farmyard and with a view of the trees and the crows which she would have been happier without. It was a small, cold room, but she had little time to spend in it. Her days were long hectic rounds of domestic and farm routines. The Lynches kept other staff, but not enough, and there was always something to be done.

At first, Sally Rua was not unhappy. Mrs Lynch was a reasonable woman who wanted her servants to be contented, if for no other reason than she would get more out of them in that way. She spoke Irish to them, since she knew they preferred it, and to her children, because really she felt more at home in that language herself, even though the doctor, from Letterkenny, wished English to be the language of his household. That did not matter: he was not often at home, and never in the kitchen where Sally Rua spent most of the time when she was not in the byre or the dairy. When she described her life in Rathmullan to her mother, whom she visited once a month, she painted a picture of a calm, contented existence.

This description began to change after about three months. Sally Rua, speaking in a voice which had become low and monotone and should itself have been a warning to her mother, said she was anxious. Her mother, legs parted to catch the heat of the flames, looked at her – anxiously – shook her head and did not pursue the matter. Sally Rua, lying that night on her high bed in Rathmullan, watching the shadows of the giant oak trees gloom across the floor, wept. She told herself she was stupid. She told herself she was sad. She told herself she was miserable, lonely.

What she was missing was the house at Wavesend, her sisters, her friends. Her mother. Homesick she was. She had been homesick from day one. But there was more to it than that. What really made her cry with misery and frustration was the way she was missing her work. Her real work. The flowering.

She had hoped, at first, that there would be some need for that here. That Mrs Lynch would ask her to make some antimacassars for her big armchairs and sofa, which could badly do with them, or runners for the dressing tables and sideboard. After about six weeks she realized that such requests would not be forthcoming. There was plenty of needlework to be done in the Lynch household, all right, but it took the form of mending sheets and underwear and night-gowns, rather than of anything elaborate. Sally Rua was expected to spend every night working at the linen closet and wardrobe of Mrs Lynch and her daughters. She had been employed chiefly for her skills in this line; the other work she spent twelve hours a day doing was simply thrown in as a little extra.

There was, of course, no possibility of doing embroidery in her own room during her spare time, simply because she had no spare time. Every minute in the Lynch household that was not spent sleeping or eating had to be devoted to Lynch work. The only free time she had was one Sunday a month, the Sunday she spent visit-ing her mother. She did a bit of flowering while she was at home, occasionally. But a few hours a month were insufficient. There was never time to get even one flower finished, never mind a whole picture.

Sally Rua became more and more miserable. She also became more and more cross. She snapped at the other maids and at the lads in the yard, and even at Emma and Louise, the daughters of the house. Gradually her personality was transformed and she became renowned for her bad temper as she had once been renowned for her skill at the flowering. She became so crotchety that sometimes on her day off she did not go to Wavesend at all, but wandered around Rathmullan, staring at the ruined abbey, at the boats moving across the shadowy lough to Buncrana, and at the seagulls wheeling over it. She stared at the crows who built their nests in the high, scrawny oaks that surrounded the Lynch's house.

Once, on a winter's evening, when the moon was a full white circle behind the skeletal trees, she saw a hare on the fence that divided the garden from the bog. Its coat of fur was brown and gold and yellow and purple, streaked with odd white patches. It had a small white bun of a tail. Never had she seen a hare at such close quarters. She was so near that she could see its tawny eyes gazing at her, and its split trembling lip.

For minutes she stared, and all the time the hare stayed as still as the fence it sat on. Then something happened. A twig fell, a scrap of cloud shadowed the moon. And at that same moment, the hare and Sally moved. She bent, picked up a stone, and flung it hard at the hare's white tail. Before she had stooped to the ground, before she had touched the stone, the hare was gone, bounding over the moonlit turf at a hundred miles an hour.

A few days later, Sally screamed at Mrs Lynch. Mrs Lynch had simply asked her to make a white dress for Louise's confirmation, and had suggested that she do a little embroidery on the cuffs and collar. It was the first time such a request had been made. Daisies, she suggested, might be appropriate. Sally Rua had taken the material, a couple of yards of white silk, and thrown it into the fire. She watched it going up in flames without a word or a cry, and then, as Mrs Lynch, having got over her shock, began to remonstrate, she picked up all the cushions and tablecloths and textiles that were lying about the room (the drawing room) and pitched them on the fire as well. At this point she began to scream. This helped Mrs Lynch to regain her presence of mind, and she ran for help to the kitchen. John, the hired man, and Bridget the cook caught Sally Rua and pinned her down to the sofa, while someone was sent for the doctor. There was a certain gratification in imprisoning Sally Rua in this way; it was a slight revenge for all the abuse she had heaped on them over the past months.

There was no lunatic asylum in Letterkenny then, as there is now. But there was a poor house, with a wing for those of unsound mind, and that is where Sally Rua went. Later it became a lunatic asylum and she experienced that, too, for two decades before her death. She reached the age of seventy-six, and was completely mad for most of her life.

Sally Rua. She went mad because she could not do the work she loved, because she could not do her flowering. That can happen. You can love some kind of work so much that you go crazy if you simply cannot manage to do it at all. Outer or inner constraints could be the cause. Sally Rua had only outer ones. She was so good at flowering, she was such a genius at it, that she never had any inner problems. That was the good news, as far as she was concerned.

Sally Rua. Lennie's ancestor. Of course, none of that is true. It is a yarn, spun out of thin air. Not quite out of thin air: Lennie read about a woman like Sally Rua. She had read, in a history of embroidery in Ireland, about a woman who had gone mad because she could not afford to keep up the flowering which she loved, and had to go into service in a town house in the north of Ireland. The bare bones of a story. How much of that, even, is true? She might have gone mad anyway. She might have been congenitally conditioned to craziness. Or the madness might have had some other cause, quite unconnected with embroidery. The son of the house might have raped her. Or the father. Or the grandfather or the hired man. People go mad for lots of reasons, but not often for the reason that they haven't got the time to do embroidery.

Still and all. The woman who wrote the history of embroidery, an excellent, an impassioned book, the name of which would be cited if this were a work of scholarship and not a story, believed that that was the cause of the tragedy. And Lennie believes it. Because she wants to. She also wants to adopt that woman, that woman who was not, in history, called Sally Rua, but some other, less interesting name (Sally Rua really was the name of Lennie's great-grandmother, but what she knows about her is very slight), as her ancestor. Because she does not see much difference between history and fiction, between painting and embroidery, between either of them and literature. Or scholarship. Or building houses. The energies inspiring all of these endeavours cannot be so separate, after all. The essential skills of learning to manipulate the raw material, to transform it into something orderly and expressive, to make it, if not better or more beautiful, different from what it was originally and more itself, apply equally to all of these exercises. Exercises that Lennie likes to perform. Painting and writing, embroidering and scholarship. If she likes these things, someone back there in Wavesend must have liked them too. And if someone back there in Wavesend did not, if there was no Sally Rua, at all, at all, where does that leave Lennie?

3

MIDWIFE TO THE FAIRIES

We were looking at the *Late Late*. It wasn't much good this night, there was a fellow from Russia, a film star or an actor or something – I'd never heard tell of him – and some young one from America who was after setting up a prostitutes' hotel or call-in service or something. God, what Gay wants with that kind I don't know. All done up really snazzy, mind you, like a model or a television announcer or something. And she made a mint out of it, writing a book about her experiences if you don't mind. I do have to laugh!

I don't enjoy it as much of a Friday. It was much better of a Saturday. After the day's work and getting the bit of dinner ready for myself and Joe, sure I'm barely ready to sit down when it's on. It's not as relaxing like. I don't know, I do be all het up somehow on Fridays on account of it being such a busy day at the hospital and all, with all the cuts you really have to earn your keep there nowadays!

Saturday is busy too of course – we have to go into Bray and do the bit of shopping like; and do the bit of hoovering and washing. But it's not the same, I feel that bit more relaxed, I suppose it's on account of not being at work really. Not that I'd want to change that or anything. No way. Sixteen years of being at home was more than enough for me. That's not to say, of course, that I minded it at the time. I didn't go half-cracked the way some of them do, or let on to do. Mind you, I've no belief in that pre-menstrual tension and post-natal depression and what have you. I come across it often enough, I needn't tell you, or I used to, I should say, in the course of my duty. Now with the maternity unit gone, of course all that's changed. It's an ill wind, as they say. I'll say one thing for male patients, there's none of this depression carry-on with them. Of course they all think they're dying, oh dying, of sore toes and colds in the head and anything at all, but it's easier to put up with than the post-natals. I'm telling no lie.

Well, anyway, we were watching Gaybo and I was out in the kitchen wetting a cup of tea, which we like to have around ten or so of a Friday. Most nights we wait till it's nearer bedtime, but on Fridays I usually do have some little treat I get on the way home from work in The Hot Bread Shop there on the corner of Corbawn Lane, in the new shopping centre. Some little extra, a few Danish pastries or doughnuts, some little treat like that. For a change more than anything. This night I'd a few Napoleons – you know, them cream slices with icing on top.

I was only after taking out the plug when the bell went. Joe answered it of course and I could hear him talking to whoever it was and I wondered who it could be at that hour. All the stories you hear about burglars and people being murdered in their own homes . . . there was a woman over in Dalkey not six months ago, hacked to pieces at ten o'clock in the morning. God help her! . . . I do be worried. Naturally. Though I keep the chain on all the time and I think that's the most important thing. As long as you keep the chain across you're all right. Well, anyway, I could hear them talking and I didn't go out. And after a few minutes I could hear him taking the chain off and letting whoever it was in. And then Joe came in to me and he says:

'There's a fellow here looking for you, Mary. He says it's urgent.'

'What is it he wants? Sure I'm off duty now anyway, amn't I?'

I felt annoyed, I really did. The way people make use of you! You'd think there was no doctors or something. I'm supposed to be a nurse's aide, to work nine to five, Monday to Friday, except when I'm on nights. But do you think the crowd around here can get that into their heads? No way.

'I think you'd better have a word with him yourself, Mary. He says it's urgent like. He's in the hail.'

I knew of course. I knew before I seen him or heard what he had to say. And I took off my apron and ran my comb through my hair to be ready. I made up my own mind that I'd have to go out

with him in the cold and the dark and miss the rest of the *Late Late*.
But I didn't let on of course.

*There was a handywoman in this part of the country and she used to be
called out at all times of the day and night. But one night a knock came to
her door. The woman got up at once and got ready to go out. There was a
man standing at the door with a mare.*

He was a young fellow with black hair, hardly more than eighteen
or nineteen.

'Well,' says I, 'what's your trouble?'

'It's my wife,' he said, embarrassed like. He'd already told Joe, I
don't know what he had to be embarrassed about. Usually you'd get
used to a thing like that. But anyway he was, or let on to be.

'She's expecting. She says it's on the way.

'And who might you be?'

'I'm her husband.' Didn't believe in names. Oh well.

'I see,' says I. And I did. I didn't come down in the last shower.
And with all the carry-on that goes on around here you'd want to
be thick or something not to get this particular message straight
away. But I didn't want to be too sure of myself. Just in case.
Because, after all, you can never be too sure of anything in this life.
'And why?' says I to him then, 'Why isn't she in hospital, where she
should be?'

'There isn't time,' he said, as bold as brass.

'Well,' says I then, 'closing maternity wards won't stop them having babies.' I laughed, trying to be a bit friendly like. But he didn't
see the joke. So, says I, 'And where do you and your wife live?'

'We live on this side of Annamoe,' he said, 'and if you're coming
we'd better be off. It's on the way, she said.'

'I'll come,' I said. What else could I say? A call like that has to be
answered. My mother did it before me and her mother before her,
and they never let anyone down. And my mother said that her
mother had never lost a child. Not one. Her corporate works of
mercy, she called it. You get indulgence. And anyway I pitied him, he
was only a young fellow and he was nice-looking, too, he had a

country look to him. But of course I was under no obligation, none whatever, so I said, 'Not that I should come really. I'm off duty, you know, and anyway what you need is the doctor.'

'We'd rather have you,' he said.

'Well, just this time.'

'Let's go then!'

'Hold on a minute, I'll get the keys of the car from Joe.'

'Oh, sure I'll run you down and back, don't bother about your own car.'

'Thank you very much,' I said. 'But I'd rather take my own, if it's all the same to you. I'll follow on behind you.' You can't be too careful.

So I went out to start the car. But lo and behold, it wouldn't go! Don't ask me why, that car is nearly new. We got it last winter from Mike Byrne, my cousin that has the garage outside Greystones. There's less than thirty thousand miles on her and she was serviced only there a month before Christmas. But it must have been the cold or something. I tried, and he tried, and Joe, of course, tried, and none of us could get a budge out of her. So in the heel of the hunt I'd to go with him. Joe didn't want me to, and then he wanted to come himself, and your man . . . Sean O'Toole, he said his name was . . . said OK, OK, but come on quick. So I told Joe to get back inside to the fire and I went with him. He'd an old Cortina, a real old banger, a real farmer's car.

'Do not be afraid!' said the rider to her. 'I will bring you home to your own doorstep tomorrow morning!'

She got up behind him on the mare.

Neither of us said a word the whole way down. The engine made an awful racket, you couldn't hear a thing, and anyway he was a quiet fellow with not a lot to say for himself. All I could see were headlights, and now and then a signpost: Enniskerry, Sallygap, Glendalough. And after we turned off the main road into the mountains, there were no headlights either, and no house-lights, nothing except the black night. Annamoe is at the back of beyonds, you'd never know you were only ten miles from Bray there, it's really very remote altogether. And their house was down a lane where there was absolutely nothing to be seen at all, not a house, not even a sheep. The house you could hardly see either, actually. It was kind of buried like at the side of the road, in a kind of a hollow. You wouldn't know it was there at all until you were on top of it. Trees all around it too. He pulled up in front of a big five-bar gate and just gave an almighty honk on the horn, and I got a shock when the gate opened, just like that, the minute he honked. I never saw who did it. But looking back now I suppose it was one of the brothers. I suppose they were waiting for him like.

It was a big place, comfortable enough, really, and he took me into the kitchen and introduced me to whoever was there. Polite enough. A big room it was, with an old black range and a huge big dresser, painted red and filled with all kinds of delph and crockery and stuff. Oh you name it! And about half a dozen people were sitting around the room, or maybe more than that. All watching the telly. The *Late Late* was still on and your one, the call-girl one, was still on. She was talking to a priest about unemployment. And they were glued to it, the whole lot of them, what looked like the mother and father and a whole family of big grown men and women. His family or hers I didn't bother my head asking. And they weren't giving out information for nothing either. It was a funny set up, I could see that as clear as daylight, such a big crowd of them, all living together. For all the world like in *Dallas*.

Well, there wasn't a lot of time to be lost. The mother offered me a cup of tea, I'll say that for her, and I said yes, I'd love one, and I was actually dying for a cup. I hadn't had a drop of tea since six o'clock and by this time it was after twelve. But I said I'd have a look at the patient first. So one of them, a sister I suppose it was, the youngest of them, she took me upstairs to the room where she was. The girl. Sarah. She was lying on the bed, on her own. No heat in the room, nothing.

After a while they came to a steep hill. A door opened in the side of the hill and they went in. They rode until they came to a big house and inside there were lots of people, eating and drinking. In a corner of the house there lay a woman in labour.

I didn't say a word, just put on the gloves and gave her the examination. She was the five fingers, nearly into the second stage, and she
must have been feeling a good bit of pain but she didn't let on, not
at all. Just lay there with her teeth gritted. She was a brave young
one, I'll say that for her. The waters were gone and of course
nobody had cleaned up the mess so I asked the other young one to
do it, and to get a heater and a kettle of boiling water. I stayed with
Sarah and the baby came just before one. A little girl. There was no
trouble at all with the delivery and she seemed all right but small.
I'd no way of weighing her, needless to say, but I'd be surprised if
she was much more than five pounds.

'By rights she should be in an incubator,' I said to Sarah, who was
sitting up smoking a cigarette, if you don't mind. She said nothing.
What can you do? I washed the child . . . she was a nice little thing,
God help her . . . I wrapped her in a blanket and put her in beside
the mother. There was nowhere else for her. Not a cot, not even an
old box. That's the way in these cases as often as not. Nobody wants
to know.

I delivered the afterbirth and then I left. I couldn't wait to get
back to my own bed. They'd brought me the cup of tea and all, but
I didn't get time to drink it, being so busy and all. And afterwards
the Missus, if that's what she was, wanted me to have a cup in the
kitchen. But all I wanted then was to get out of the place. They
were all so quiet and unfriendly like. Bar the mother. And even she
wasn't going overboard, mind you. But the rest of them. All sitting
like zombies looking at the late-night film. They gave me the
creeps. I told them the child was too small, they'd have to do something about it, but they didn't let on they heard. The father, the ould
fellow, that is to say, put a note in my hand . . . it was worth it from
that point of view, I'll admit . . . and said, 'Thank you.' Not a word
from the rest of them. Glued to the telly, as if nothing was after happening. I wanted to scream at them, really. But what could I do?
Anyway the young fellow, Sean, the father as he said himself, drove
me home. And that was that.

Well and good. I didn't say a word about what was after happening
to anyone, excepting of course to Joe. I don't talk, it's not right.
People have a right to their privacy, I always say, and with my calling
you've to be very careful. But to tell the truth they were on my

mind. The little girl, the little baby. I knew in my heart and soul I shouldn't have left her out there, down there in the back of beyonds, near Annamoe. She was much too tiny, she needed care. And the mother, Sarah, was on my mind as well. Mind you, she seemed to be well able to look after herself, but still and all, they weren't the friendliest crowd of people I'd ever come across. They were not.

But that was that.

Until about a week later, didn't I get the shock of my life when I opened the evening paper and saw your one, Sarah, staring out at me. Her round baby face, big head of red hair. And there was a big story about the baby. Someone was after finding it dead in a shoe-box, in a kind of rubbish dump they had at the back of the house. And she was arrested, in for questioning, her and maybe Sean O'Toole as well. I'm not sure. In for questioning. I could have dropped down dead there and then.

I told Joe.

'Keep your mouth shut, woman,' he said. 'You did your job and were paid for it. This is none of your business.'

And that was sound advice. But we can't always take sound advice. If we could the world would be a different place.

The thing dragged on. It was in the papers. It was on the telly. There was questioning, and more questioning, and trials and appeals and I don't know what. The whole country was in on it.

And it was on my conscience. It kept niggling at me all the time. I couldn't sleep, I got so I couldn't eat. I was all het up about it, in a terrible state really. Depressed, that's what I was, me who was never depressed before in my life. And I'm telling no lie when I say I was on my way to the doctor for a prescription for Valium when I realized there was only one thing to do. So instead of going down to the surgery, didn't I turn on my heel and walk over to the Garda barracks instead. I went in and I got talking to the sergeant straight away. Once I told them what it was about there was no delaying. And he was very interested in all I had to say, of course, and asked me if I'd be prepared to testify and I said of course I would. Which was the truth. I wouldn't want to but I would if I had to. Once I'd gone this far, of course I would.

Well, I walked out of that Garda station a new woman. It was a great load off my chest. It was like being to confession and getting absolution for a mortal sin. Not that I've ever committed a mortler, of course. But you know what I mean. I felt relieved.

Well and good.

Well. You'll never believe what happened to me next. I was just getting back to my car when a young fellow . . . I'd seen him somewhere before, I know that, but I couldn't place him. He might have been the fellow that came for me on the night, Sean, but he didn't look quite like him. I just couldn't place him at all . . . anyway, he was standing there, right in front of the car. And I said hello, just in case I really did know him, just in case it really was him. But he said nothing. He just looked behind him to see if anyone was coming, and when he saw that the coast was clear he just pulled out a big huge knife out of his breast pocket and pointed it at my stomach. He put the heart crossways in me. And then he says, in a real low voice, like a gangster in *Hill Street Blues* or something:

'Keep your mouth shut. Or else!'

I was in bits. I could hardly drive myself home with the shock. I told Joe of course. But he didn't have a lot of sympathy for me.

'God Almighty, woman,' he said, 'what possessed you to go to the guards? You must be off your rocker. They'll be arresting you next!'

Well, I'd had my lesson. The guards called for me the next week but I said nothing. I said I knew nothing and I'd never heard tell of them all before, the family I mean. And there was nothing they could do, nothing. The sergeant hadn't taken a statement from me, and that was his mistake and my good luck I suppose, because I don't know what would have happened to me if I'd testified. I told a priest about the lie to the guards, in confession, to a Carmelite in White Friar Street, not to any priest I know. And he said God would understand. 'You did your best, and that's all God will ask of you. He does not ask of us that we put our own lives in danger.'

There was a fair one day at Baile an Droichid. And this woman used to make market socks and used to wash them and scour them and take them to the fair and get them sold. She used to make them up in dozen bunches and sell them at so much the dozen.

And as she walked over the bridge there was a great blast of wind. And who should it be but the people of the hill, the wee folk! And she looked among them and saw among them the same man who had taken her on the mare's back to see his wife.

'How are ye all? And how is the wife?' she said.

He stood and looked at her.

'Which eye do you see me with?' he asked.

'With the right eye,' she said.

Before he said another word he raised his stick and stuck it in her eye and knocked her eye out on the road.

'You'll never see me again as long as you live,' he said.

Sometimes I do think of the baby. She was a dawny little thing, there's no two ways about it. She might have had a chance, in intensive care. But who am I to judge?

4

THE WIFE OF BATH

We're in the Roman baths at Bath. Well, not actually in them, most of us, because we take heed of the sign at the edge of the pool letting us know that the water is not fit for drinking or bathing in, because it hasn't been treated. It's oilskin green, the water, and steaming in the winter air. All around are antique pillars, beige and terracotta, comfortable and crumbly as fresh digestive biscuits. All around are tourists, French and Swedish and Japanese, emitting small polite sounds, pretty perfumes. Discreet dismay. Controlled disapproval. Of Johnny.

He's on the first step, stooping to test the water with his grubby paw. He's on the second step, splashing. He's on the third, where the water is reasonably deep, and where he therefore thinks it opportune to paddle. His small face is concentrated and stern.

Disgust. Plain as Medusa's moon face, which is graven on a rock at the side of the bath, is painted on all the Gorgon visages, pink, black, yellow, white, emerging from the furry collars of their winter raincoats, peering from beneath their felt, astrakhan, squirrel, fox, hair hats.

It's turned Jim to stone. And no wonder.

So it is I who pull Johnny out. And no wonder.

'Johnny!' I don't shout, I whisper. It's not a church but you feel that sound is sacrilegious here, it's all so ancient, so nice. Bath seems so frightfully bloody nice.

'Johnny, how could you!'

'He looks nonplussed, uncomprehending, and indeed the question is rhetorical. Why wouldn't he? Put his feet in a pool of deliciously hot water? The water is not two thousand years old, after

31

all. It's a few minutes old, young and mischievous; it springs boiling and bubbling, full of its own power, full of its own salts, full of its own bubble bath for all I know, from the ground. In other less refined parts of the world where the crust of the earth is thinner and younger than in England people swim in this kind of thing, they use it as a public jacuzzi, they wash their clothes in it. Besides, Johnny always does what he feels like doing: plays the piano in a bar, if it happens to contain a piano; swings out of velvet curtains, rushes on to the altars of cathedrals, shouting and singing, effervescent as a fountain, frisky as a lamb. Why wouldn't he paddle in a pool?

He's not even dripping wet. It's just his feet, which happen to be encased in rubber wellington boots. It's as if he knew and had prepared in advance. But this can hardly be the case. It's just one of those miraculous fortuities sometimes used as proof of God's existence, like the increased proportion of male births following great political catastrophes. How terrible, to have been a mother in 1947, when the world was apparently full of little naughty boys, hardly a girl in sight, if you believe the statistics.

'How could you!'

The gorgons have released Jim. He's now disgorging emotions, of some sort. What sort? Shame, anger, pain, hatred, fear? They are not positive, that's all one knows, springing up, sulphurous, hellish, splashing out haphazardly over me and Johnny, whom he tends to regard as a unit, like splutters from a kettle, sparks from a firecracker. Sulphur sulphur everywhere and not a drop to drink.

'Johnny, how could you!'

Drink the oilskin filth. God, he'll be sick after this or we're all monkey's uncles. Untreated hot water, two thousand years old, two million years old. How could he!

I met her in a pub. The Hop Pole Inn, it's called. It's in Limpley Stoke, five miles from the centre of the town. She was fat, of course, but that sort of fat which is fertile and attractive, not the morbid sad kind. Pleasantly plump, people used to say, in the old days before health and anorexia came in. She'd a denim skirt, tight and certainly short for someone with such thick thighs, red tights, a red sweater, the long loose kind that's fashionable now and always among students but not so much among forty year olds. Only hers was not all that loose; it left not too much to the imagination. Her hair was dyed blond, sticking out around her head in yellow spikes from under a navy blue bandana type of thing. She was drinking a pint, at the bar.

And what was I doing? I was alone, pussyfooting across the threshold, cat creeping into the inn, cavilling, apologising. To whom? There was nobody there; it must have been to myself. But then, I had a dim suspicion that something or somebody was missing, that I'd mislaid a thought or a time or a person, but I was damned if I could remember what. I'm getting so absent minded! Yes, I eat half a banana a day for the potassium, which is great for the memory, preventing or staving off senility in most, but not, apparently, in me. What those bananas do for me is, they make me fat.

'Yes love?' she turned to me, and I realised she was the barmaid, after all, though on the wrong side of it.

'A pint of bitter.'

What do you mean, you don't drink pints, and you don't drink bitter? As a matter of fact, you don't really know what bitter is, except in the north of Germany where it's definitely something else, and plural, and if it were that or them you would most certainly not order it.

She heaved herself off the stool and went in behind the counter, drawing a pint of oaky liquid in a few seconds. So efficient, so quick, so much less a pain in the ass than the beer I'm used to.

'On holiday then?'

'Yes,' I said, after a pause. And then, remembering Johnny, I added, 'What's a holiday?'

She answered nonchalantly, 'Search me. I've never had one, as such. Pilgrimages, voyages, yes. Holidays, no. But anyway, welcome to beside Bath.' And she came back outside. 'What's your name?'

'Oh!' I paused again. 'Maureen,' I said, 'I think.' It was the first name that came into my head, because, when I was three, the girl who lived in the house next door, and was five and tall as a tree and lovely, was called Maureen. She had long hair, brown in colour, and ate nothing except celery. All this I knew. But not my own name.

'I'm Alisoun.'

'Hello, Dame Alisoun.'

'They call me . . .'

'I know, I know.' And I did. 'Tell me, have you always kept a pub?'

'No, of course not. I didn't need to, in the old days. Merry England. I had a husband to support me then.'

'One husband?'

'Five, ten, a hundred. What does it matter? They don't support me any more. So I run a pub: don't own it, naturally. I'm just the manageress.'

'It should suit you! You've the personality for the job, I'd guess.'

'Oh, sure! Jolly matronly type, that's me. I can do it as well as the next, but the fact is, it doesn't suit me at all. What I fancy is, ambling around on a stout mare, going on trips abroad or at home. Having a chat.'

'You can have chats here though, can't you?'

'In between the washing up, I can. I used to leave all that side of it to Bert. But poor old Bert, he . . .'

'Kicked the can.'

'Yes. Poor old Bert!'

'You should get a dishwasher.'

'I have already. Just like a husband, it is. Does all the easy things and leaves the messy ones for me.'

'Hm. Tell me,' I settled myself comfortably in my seat, which was a deep tweed cushion. 'Tell me about Jankyn. What happened in the end, to him and you?'

'I'd nearly forgotten about him. It's such a while ago.'

'He was a student.'

'A clerk, he was, of Oxenforde. Is that the one you mean? You know him?'

'Sort of. He's written a lot about the Church Fathers.'

'Yeah, he was a great one for the books, old Jankyn. Or young Jankyn, I should say. Cor, he was half my age, even then. But nice hair he'd got. I fell for his hair, and put up with the books for the sake of that.'

'I thought you fell for his legs.'

'Oh, them too, them too! Men's legs, my word! I haven't seen legs like those in three hundred year or so . . . at least it feels that long. They're out of fashion. Such a pity.'

'I can't agree, I, must say.' And I considered legs, white, black-haired, skinny, and white, blackhaired, fat. Grey-white like flour and water paste.

'They weren't the same, the legs I knew. Oh no, not at all. You know men's legs now, how they're thin and all? It's from covering 'em up all the time. If men had their legs out, like we do, they'd be a lot fatter, they would. They used to be much fatter.'

'Even his?'

'His weren't so much fat as shapely. That's what I liked about 'em, actually, as he walked up the aisle.'

I could see the legs then, golden brown, covered with fine hair that the sun danced on, the way sun dances onto drops of water, on little summer waves. The legs walked along an aisle, disembodied.

'Was that in the Abbey?'

That was it. On the altar, Johnny, fat round legs in blue jeans, screaming: 'I just want to touch it, touch it, touch it! Let me touch it!'

'Naw, it weren't in the abbey, at least not that one you're talking about, beside the Pump Room and all. Lor, no, I wouldn't have been seen dead in that neighbourhood, even then. There weren't no pump room then, of course, not that prissy place they have now. No baths, no abbey, nothing like that. Just a nice little tavern and a few washerwomen, very civilised really. I can't stand that place now.'

'It's a bit Jane Austeny.'

'You can say that again. One woman I never could take, Jane Austen. Silly bitch. Man crazy.

'She seems less interested in them than you were, in all fairness,' said I.

Well, maybe I should 'ave said, she was husband mad. The only thing in life was husbands, as far as she was concerned, and she never even got one.'

Weren't you obsessed with husbands yourself.'

'I was more interested in getting rid of them. Because I had them, one two three four five, once I caught a fish alive. I knew what they were like. Not Jane. It was all pie in the sky as far as she was concerned.'

'At least, she did write and analyse the situation a bit.'

There is somewhere a pen rusty, an inkwell dry, a quire of paper lying unopened in a drawer. Did I read of it, did I see it, is it mine? Or some other woman's? Or every woman's?

'So bloody what? Jankyn wrote. Whenever he wasn't reading he was writing. That was the trouble with him!'

'Remember what you said: if women wrote stories they'd write such wicked things of men.'

'I would.'

'I would too.'

We laughed together. Her mouth opened in a huge guffaw, the kind women who have made it, who no longer give a straw, who are themselves alone, have. Some are born with it, some acquire it. A rare trait either way.

'Are you married?' she asked.

'Oh yes, I believe so.'

'It's better, in the long run, really. It's an experience.'

'It's difficult for me. I'm a feminist.'

'Well, I don't see what that has to do with the price of eggs. I am too, always was, not like Jane Austen.'

'Oh, I don't know if you were, really. I think there are those who'd dispute that.'

'Bloody fools they are.'

'You depended on men rather a lot. I mean, one husband is more than enough for most feminists. But five? God; Elizabeth Taylor is hardly a feminist . . . you're more like her.'

'Like hell I am!' She uncrossed her ample legs and stood, feet apart, on the floor. 'I had no choice, you see, that's the difference. What could I have been? I couldn't read or write, like Jankyn, I couldn't star in the movies, I couldn't, really, at that time, manage a public house. Fact is, I couldn't do anything except part my legs on a horse or in bed. And I did that to the best of my ability.'

'You were good at embroidery, I believe.'

She gave me a crafty look.

'Yes, I was. But I did it for pleasure, pure pleasure. It was my art, embroidery, I passeth 'em of Ypres and of Ghent, but I didn't bloody want to wear out my eyesight doing it and selling it for half nothing to ignoramuses who couldn't tell the difference beween guipure and appliqué. Do you know anything about needlework?'

'Well . . .' No. Not needlework. The point in, the point out, dragging and pulling endless threads. To make, not create. I think I must be different. I am impatient, I want to make new things. To weave perhaps? Weave what? Am I a weaver? Maureen the weaver. Is that who I am?

'The main thing about embroidery, all embroidery, is that it's a great craft and it's always undervalued. I needn't tell you why.'

'No.'

'So, who'd try to kill themselves embroidering? Marriage was easier, in the end, and much more lucrative. Let's be honest. Let's call a spade a spade.'

'Jane Austen did. And Jankyn.'

'Jankyn thought he was smarter than me. But he got his comeuppance, as you know. I got everything back, finally, and he was glad to give it to me. And I got rid of him, too.'

'How?'

'That was always easy. They all went, you know, on crusades or whatever, you know; that was how I got shut of them as a rule. But Jankyn, he actually died of jealousy.

'Really? Isn't that rather unusual? I don't mean to be offensive . . .'

'Not of me. One of the drawbacks of the academic life. Another clerke at Oxford got a promotion Jankyn thought he deserved. Because of contacts, you know, the olde storye. Poor Jankyn. He was learned but not very wise, and he couldn't take it. He went mad and then he died.'

'But you married again.'

'Time and time again.'

'That's what I can't understand, really. You knew what it was like. It had always been full of problems. You didn't need the money or anything, but you kept on marrying. Why on earth?'

'Well, I like sex, that was one reason. The main reason . . . and the Next, the Next always seems the best.

Jankyn walking down the aisle, young with good legs, fair hair . . . you know what I mean?'

'Yes.'

Yes. Polygamy is the strongest instinct. Especially in women. Next is Best.

'Like another pint?'

I had another pint. My head was misted over, steaming. From the fog shadows emerged and then went right back again. A golden legged man, for whom I felt huge surges of desire for seconds, until he vanished. And other men for whom I felt no desire, except to know their names.

'And then, there's the battlefield aspect. For the sex war. In the Middle Ages, my prime, so to speak, it was the only sparring ground. Different now. Women vote and belong to trade unions and women's groups and political parties. They can fight with men in all kinds of arenas. But then there was just the one old place. Bed.'

'You think it's all still about maistrye.'

Oh yes, of course. It was in my day, my olde daye, I mean, and it still is. The difference is that in the Middle Ages I had to get it within marriage ... you don't think those damn pilgrims would have listened to me if I hadn't been married?'

'They listened to the prioresse.'

'Married to Christ. Jesus, I couldn't have stood that. I need to use my instrument, as I've pointed out more than once before.'

'We used to gloss over that bit in class.'

She looked puzzled but not very, and she wasn't the sort of woman to be thrown by a misunderstandmg.

'What I mean is, I couldn't have controlled anything outside of marriage, but inside, I had some power.' She tossed her yellow head and thrust out her red breast.

'Really? My impression was that Jankyn, the one you cared about, the only one, gave you a rough time.'

'He did.' Her eyes took on a dreamy look, as she stared through a mullioned window at a dim view of the Avon.

'Hardly feminist, to put up with that!'

'No. But it was worth it. I mean, I loved him.'

'Love hadn't been invented really.'

'It had, as a matter of fact, but it hadn't got to Bath. Didn't mat-

ter though. I fancied him. He did things for me. In our bed he was
so fresh and gay!'

Our bed is wide and covered with a brown candlewick counter-
pane. The sheets are white, ironed, fresh, but hardly gay. We gaze
upon five windows, giving on a view of the Hop Pole Inn. We lie in
bed from six in the evening, when it gets dark, to six in the morning, when it is light. Jim reads his books: there are ten in his
weekend bag, and hardly anything else. Johnny watches television.
He has a bath, plays with Lego, draws pictures.

'What's that, Johnny?'

'It's a dirty nappy and wee wee pie.'

'Oh my, it's very good!'

Johnny smiles his angelic smile.

'Would you like to go to bed, Johnny?'

'Nooohh!' he screams, and I hope the hotel manager will not run
up to find out what's the matter. Jim lifts his head to scowl at both
of us and when the bloodcurdling. screech fades, bows it once more
to the seductive page.

'Were you not a bit of a masochist?'

'Yes. I was a bit of a masochist. I have to admit it . . . for a while.
And he was a bloody sadist . . . it all turned us on, let's face it . . . for
a while. In the end, I got over it, him, everything. I got what I
wanted from him.'

'Maistrye?'

'Yes.'

'It's all so futile!'

'Futile?'

'All that fighting and shouting and scheming. Just to better some
no good little clerk.'

'He was my husband. It was my life.'

'But what a waste of energy! Wouldn't it be better to use it doing
other things?'

'Like what?'

'Fighting for women's rights. Educating yourself. Writing books,
like Jane Austen;

'I hate Jane Austen. I hate all that Pump and Assembly Rooms lot
. . . prim and proper, butter wouldn't melt in my mouth types.
They're rotten through and through, much more masochistic than I
ever was.'

'But at least she did something . . . you didn't do anything. You
didn't even exist, for heaven's sake: you are just a figment of some
man's imagination, and he chose to make you a nymphomaniac, a
woman exploiting men, a shrew . . . and see, just look how you've
ended up!'

She pouted. 'See how you've ended up!' she said angrily. 'Look at
you! Tied to a husband who doesn't talk to you, who spends his
holidays with his nose in a book and has affairs with his secretary
the rest of the time, while you spend your life battling with that little brat!'

'Johnny's not a brat.'

'He is. Everybody knows that.'

'What can I do?'

She looked at me knowingly. 'There's not much. But they do
grow up.'

In the dining-room we eat breakfast in a corner, secluded, as far as
possible, from the other guests. Jim hides behind a newspaper, his
hands emerging from time to time to prong a piece of bacon or
egg, or snatch a slice of toast from the rack in the middle of the
table. Johnny grabs handfuls of cereal, eats a bit, flings the rest on the
floor. He Crawls under the table and across the room, under the
cloth of another table. He pinches an elderly lady on the thigh. She
screams and Johnny doubles up with laughter.

'Take him away!' Jim growls. I get up and take him away.

'I'm sorry, Mum,' Johnny says, in his most penitent tones. 'I didn't
know I was doing anything wrong. Can I watch TV now?'

As we walk up the shallow red stairs to our room, a frog jumps
out of Johnny's pocket and scuttles up ahead of us, fortunately taking a wrong turn on the landing. I pretend I haven't seen him.

'Did you have children?' I asked her suddenly. 'There's lots of stuff about reproduction and so on as an excuse for all the hopping in and out of bed, but there's no mention of kids. I bet you never had one in your life!' I felt triumphant. I'd got her now.

'I'd fifteen,' she said icily. 'How many have you?'

'Him.'

'Just him. All the fuss about that little whelp. I had fifteen, but I never saw them from the day of their birth until they were old enough to behave themselves like decent human beings, and not for long then either. If there's one thing I can't stand it's children.'

'Didn't it harm them, never seeing you?'

'I would have harmed them much more if they had.'

'And what became of them all?'

'Oh, I forget . . . the usual things, I suppose. Millers, sumoners, friars, pardoners, franklins, that sort of thing.'

'You never kept up contact with them?'

'They never kept in touch with me! Children never do, didn't you know?'

'Mm. I ring my mother once a month.'

'Oh, well I was so mobile. It's only recently that I've come back here, to settle down. I was a roving spirit before then. I've been a wild rover for many a year and now I'm serving up whiskey and beer.'

'You were in Jerusalem, I remember.'

'Oh, I'd love to go back! There and everywhere else.'

'I've always thought travel was so liberating.'

'Let's go on a weekend break to Bath. It's so good to get off this island, even for a few days!'

'With Johnny!' Jim's tone was sceptical. 'It'll be fine.'

'Very well, whatever you wish.'

We churned across the sea to Fishguard, we drove two hundred miles on the M4, we got lost in Limpley Stoke.

'At Limpley Stoke my heart was broke!' Johnny chanted in the back of the car.

'Can't you get him to stop? He's driving me demented.' Jim had been driving around the narrow steep lanes for more than an hour.

'Shut up, Johnny, shut up, please shut up!'

'Feel like a swim?'

'Yes, I always feel like a swim.' I lighten.

'Let's go then . . . I can't swim, but I like to bathe.'

'I'll teach you. It's easy as cheese,' I said.

We got up on her broad-backed mare and ambled at a smart pace into the centre of Bath. The crowds were there, the sweet-smelling well-dressed hordes, milling into the museum, queuing up to drink tea in the pump room, nodding and smiling, bowing and scraping. I thought I saw Catherine Morley there, I thought I saw Isabel, and a chill descended, momentarily, a deathly fear of doing wrong, putting a foot wrong, not minding my p's and q's.

'Pints and Quarts!' yelled the wife of Bath. 'We're in!' And we dived, dove, jumped, into the hot natural baths, the crowds cooed oohed aahed and disappeared and I struck out across the pool. Oh how I love to swim. It dissolves me, it absolves me, it frees my heart and my mind and my soul, above all my soul it frees.

'Alisoun, Alisoun, do not droun!'

'I'm dissolving,' she said, 'I am,' and she was. Bits of her were melting away, as if she were made of baked sugar or something which couldn't last in water.

'Get out, good wife, before you're gone!' I cried. 'Get out.'

'No no, I can't, it's too lovely! Look, you're dissolving too, you soon won't exist, and you did once, not like me. I was just one man's invention. I'm made of parchment. I can't last in water. But you, you're real, and you're going too. It's something in this water . . . Look at the way it bubbles . . . You better get out, get out while you have a chance!'

'Does it matter?'

'Does it matter? Does it matter? Does it matter?' The question echoed around the ancient crumbling edifice, bounced off the walls, resounded delightfully in my ear, like some lovely symphony of heavenly sounds. Aqua Sulis: it lapped over me, over her, the Wife of Bath, and we melted away, feet, legs, bottoms, tummys, breasts, one by one.

'Look, you're three quarters gone!'

Suddenly Jim and Johnny flashed across my line of vision. Then I had a momentary realisation of whom I was, what I was, of the privileges and duties that I should bear. But they were all disappearing. There was no weight in the pack anymore. I could see only Johnny and Jim as a whirl of limbs, golden, gliding, in the warm stream rising from the warm water, the water which lifted the gravity from every mortal thing, which bore away everything with liquid ease, as I melted, laughing, into the sacred spring.

5

THE CATECHISM EXAMINATION

Something about the way the garden hedge looks today gives me a feeling I would have difficulty in describing, although I recognize it very well. I had this feeling before, as a child. Perhaps since then too. But I only recall the first time.

The hedge, let me say, is very still. A quiet, neat line, separating the garden from the road. At the far side of the road is a stone wall, and beyond that the sea, which is an even grey colour, with dark flecks where the waves dip. The sky is the same colour as the sea, only a little lighter. No seagulls, no garden birds, no dogs, are visible. Just lines, grey and dark grey and black. It is a foggy day, dull, and lovely.

We were to have our catechism examination. For three months, ever since the Christmas holidays, Miss O'Byrne had been drilling us in the two hundred and thirty questions we, as prospective First-Communicants, were expected to know. We learned five questions every night for the first two months, and then we revised ten a night during the month before the exam. Even the most stupid girl in the class, Mary Doyle, knew nearly all the answers by now.

Miss O'Byrne is a strict teacher. That is her reputation, what the big girls and the mothers say about her. And she lives up to it. She even looks strict: tall, with angular features and menacing butterfly glasses. The frames of her glasses are transparent, but the wings are brilliant royal blue, with diamonds glittering in the corners. Behind, above, her eyes sparkle, sharp and penetrating.

She strides in every morning, her thin legs pushing against her black pencil skirt. The first thing she does is call the roll. When a name is called and no one answers she glares at each face in turn, creating a palpable thrill of excitement in the big Georgian drawing room. Her eye rests, briefly, on me, and I feel afraid, and oddly pleased. Am I to be punished because, say, Mary Clarke is absent? She does not sit beside me, I have nothing much to do with her, I don't even like her. But Miss O'Byrne's ways are mysterious to me, and to all of us. Her system, if she has one, is not something we understand.

She looks down at the roll-book and we watch her fountain pen, a special Parker kept for performing this important task, scratch a big 'x' beside the name of the absentee. Miss O'Byrne smiles to herself, and shakes her head. Then she blots the roll-book with her pink blotter and the day begins.

Who made the world? Who is God? Who are the three persons of the Blessed Trinity? What is meant by Transubstantiation? What are the Ten Commandments? The Seven Deadly Sins? The Six Commandments of the Church?

Now, in the last week, she goes through all two hundred and thirty questions every day. It takes from nine o'clock until two, given the half-hour break for lunch. She begins calmly, and the class, too, is calm, at first. The girls sit upright in their narrow desks, faces pink and newly scrubbed, hair brushed back and tied in blue ribbons. Gradually the pressure increases. Girls make mistakes, and have to stand out in line to be slapped. Three slaps for each mistake. Miss O'Byrne takes this part of the proceedings seriously. She slaps using three or four rulers, bound together with an elastic band. Rumour has it that she once tried to introduce a bamboo cane, but the Parents' Committee and the Parish Priest banned it: bamboo can leave marks.

Miss O'Byrne's patience goes, soon, and order vanishes. Girls grow hot and sweaty, waiting to be asked, hoping they will survive the day without punishment, although this hardly ever happens. Their faces become red, their white blouses grow black and floppy. Only Miss O'Byrne's sweater, white angora, remains immaculate, smelling of Mum and Dior.

She takes a break to teach us a moral lesson, to tell us about the

Missions. Delighted to have a reprieve from the harrowing questioning, and eagerly anticipating the thrills to come, we sit up with suddenly renewed vigour in our desks. I run my fingers along the thick coarse grain of the wood: the wood is golden, and polished brilliantly by generations of woollen elbows, but the deep lines of its surface are filled with a black substance. It looks like fine clay, but it is dust. Ancient dust.

'Hands on your heads!' raps Miss O'Byrne, and we all obediently place our hands on the crowns of our heads. I feel my smooth hair, pulled tight downwards towards its pony tail. Underneath, my skin is hot and pulsating slightly.

The Missions. Nuns and priests and lay people who give up their lives to preach the word of God to pagans. Lay people, what are they? Some sort of hybrid, not fully human, I sense. People like Miss O'Byrne. Brave and unusual. They are killed. Tortured. She tells of pins under fingernails, tongues ripped out. I am not sure who does it, rips out the tongues. Communists, perhaps. Or black people. In Africa or China. Miss O'Byrne mentions South America but I have not heard of it before. Africa, I know all about Africa.

My arms are getting tired. I wish she would let us put them down again. When she does, the questioning will begin.

Nuns and priests and lay people are tortured, because they want to teach catechism to the pagans. And we can't learn ours properly. We are too lazy. Lazy, spoiled little city girls.

Mary Doyle is wrinkling up her face and moving her arms about dangerously. Stupid Mary Doyle. She can't learn, it seems, and she looks terrible. Small, scrawny, with thin blonde hair. Her face is white and sprinkled with freckles. Her gymslip hangs on her bony body.

She cries. Whenever she is punished, which is often, she bursts into huge uncontrollable sobs. Her pale face grows red and spotty, and her body shakes.

There is something wrong with Mary Doyle. I do not know what, but I have thought of her for some time and come to this conclusion. It irritates me, that she is on my mind. She is very often on my mind, because she is so strange, because there is something wrong with her. Why doesn't her mother do something about her?

Her mother is all right. I have seen her, sitting in the dark mildewed hall, under the statue of the Virgin: she wears a fawn teddy coat and inside her pink flowered headscarf her face is round and pleasant. Normal. Not skinny and odd. The trouble is, Mary's mother doesn't notice that her daughter is unusual. When Mary emerges from the cellar, where we hang our coats, Mrs Doyle gives her a kiss and says 'Hello lovey,' just like any other mother. Then Mary's face lights up as though there were a lamp underneath her transparent skin. And her mouth is really very big. She smiles and her whole face is taken over by the smile. She is like the Cheshire Cat my mummy reads about, at night in front of the fire in the kitchen. And even that, the way she lights up and turns into a smile, is odd. But Mrs Doyle just doesn't notice. She chats to the other mothers, about the price of First-Communion dresses and the French lessons we might get next year, as if Mary were the same as the other girls: solid, sturdy, in mind and body.

'Stop fidgeting, Mary Doyle,' says Miss O'Byrne. Mary's face wrinkles up and becomes pink. The bell rings, clanging violently through the cold gloomy rooms of the school. We are allowed to take down our hands. We are allowed to go down to the cellar, and out to our mothers, waiting in the hall.

Two days before the examination Miss O'Byrne is very nervous. Five pupils, five, are absent. During roll-call, her eyes dart about, stopping to rest for long periods now on one, now on another girl, daring those present to be absent tomorrow, or on the day of the examination itself. I feel genuinely frightened. I don't like Miss O'Byrne, but I have always trusted her not to go too far. She is an adult, she knows the limits. Today her eyes rest, for longer than is right, on me, and on others.

After roll-call, the test begins. It is a mock exam, a rehearsal for the real one, on Thursday. Tomorrow, Miss O'Byrne says, we will rest, and do no catechism. We do not believe her.

First she asks Monica Blennerhasset. Monica has thick glossy plaits, very white socks on slim legs, and a gym-slip which fits perfectly and is made of rich deep-blue serge, not the black shiny stuff which wrinkles easily, the kind I have. Monica is the best pupil. Her father is a doctor and her mother president of the Parents'

Committee, and she never misses. Usually I am disappointed when she is asked a question because the outcome is so certain, no.risks involved. Now I am relieved.

Next, she asks me. I am not like Monica Blennerhasset, or Orla O'Connor, who is the prettiest girl in the class and a champion Irish dancer. She has tiny feet, which arch like a ballerina's in her little satin pumps − we call them 'poms'. She points them exquisitely to the floor, before leaping into a star rendering of 'The Hard Reel' or 'The Double Jig'. I am not like them, a certain winner. But I am not a loser, either, and as a rule I do well enough. I know the catechism, inside out. Mummy tests me every night, in front of the fire, before she reads *Alice in Wonderland*, before bed. I can recite the answers in my sleep. I know it so well that it bores me, and I am not afraid on my own account.

After me, it is Mary Doyle's turn. She trembles as she stands up. Oh, Mary Doyle, it's stupid to tremble! Her ribbon is loose, sliding down the back of her head.

'What is the meaning of the fourth commandment of the Church?'

Mary begins: 'The meaning of the fourth commandment of the Church is . . .' Then she stops. Miss O'Byrne repeats the question.

Mary repeats: 'The meaning of the fourth commandment of the . . . of the . . . of the . . .'

She is crying already.

'Stand out,' orders Miss O'Byrne, picking up her bunch of rulers. My stomach tightens, and I feel a desire to laugh, which I suppress.

'Put out your hand.' The familiar formula has a novel quality.

Slap slap. The rulers bang together in the air, wood on wood. Then the loud smack of wood on flesh.

Six.

She would stop now.

Twelve.

Mary only missed one. Three for one. Mary is howling.

Fifteen.

Mary's sobbing has evened out, it is quieter.

Twenty.

I do not feel excited. I do not feel afraid. I want to get sick.

Twenty-three.

Mary is not howling at all. Her face is white. She is falling onto the floor.

Miss O'Byrne touches her with her foot. She wears black patent shoes with stiletto heels, very high.

'Get up, Mary Doyle,' she raps, in her cross tone. Mary does not get up.

Miss O'Byrne glares at me. I sit in the front row.

'You. Get a glass of water.'

'Yes, Miss.'

I rise immediately and leave the room. A glass of water. I have never seen a glass in the school. We bring our own plastic mugs for lunch, and pour milk into them from ketchup bottles or green triangular cartons. In winter, Maggie, the woman who cleans, gives us hot water for cocoa. The teachers drink tea from delph cups: we see them, sitting in the Teachers' Room, which overlooks the yard. They sip tea, eat sandwiches from tinfoil wrappers, and talk, as they supervise our playing.

I decide that Maggie might be in the kitchen, and go down the stone stairs to the cellar, where it is situated in a cubby-hole beside the toilets. Luckily, I find her, hunched over a little coal fire, her worn-out navy overall wrapped tightly around her body. She regards me sadly, and doesn't speak, as she hands me a cup of water. The cup is white with a green rim, the kind of cup you get on trains, and it is sinewed with thousands of barely visible veins, but it is neither cracked nor chipped.

'Did you go to the well?' Miss O'Byrne snaps. I make no response: I do not realize that her sarcasm, which is constant, is intended as humour.

Mary is sitting on a chair, her head between her knees. Thin fair hair droops onto the floorboards.

'Here, Mary, drink this.' Miss O'Byrne's voice is a catapult, the words tiny sharp stones.

Mary raises her head. Her face is whiter than ever, and her hand, when it reaches for the glass, is red, with blisters. But no blood.

'You did the ballet and passed out,' says Miss O'Byrne. Nobody knows what she is talking about.

I am standing beside Mary, waiting for the empty cup: I hope that I may be allowed to return it to the kitchen. Idly, I put my hand in my pocket, and feel there a paper tube: it is a packet of fruit pastilles, which Mummy bought for me at Mrs Dunne's, the sweetshop in the lane behind the school. Without thinking, I take the packet and hand it to Mary. Miss O'Byrne does not see what I am doing.

Mary takes the sweets and puts them into her own pocket. She does not, of course, smile, but she looks at me with her bright green eyes, shiny from all the crying, rimmed with red skin. There is a light in them, though, that lamp she has inside. Ashamed and worried by my rashness, I sit down, forgetting about the cup. When Mary stops drinking, Miss O'Byrne puts it on her table, and it is still there at two o'clock as the bell clangs and we file out to the hall.

On Thursday we are allowed to wear our own clothes. I have a red dress, nylon, with white spots. Underneath is a red silk slip, and underneath that a crinoline of stiff net, which scratches my legs but makes the skirt stand out like a lampshade, which is exactly the effect I desire.

All the girls wear their best dresses. Pink and lemon and sky blue. They all have crinolines, but nobody else has a red dress. Mummy made it for me herself, because red suits me so well.

There is an air of great excitement in the classroom, engendered by the party dresses and the prospect of the examination. Girls giggle and scream. Miss O'Byrne, in a navy suit with an emerald-green blouse, bangs her rulers against the desk, but cannot maintain order, because she has to keep running in and out of the office, talking to the other teachers, and wondering when the priest will come.

Father Harpur arrives at half past ten. His hair is grey and curly, and his face soft. On his cheek is a brown spot, a kind of mole, and when he speaks his voice is very quiet and gentle.

'Hello, girls,' he says, gazing around with a smile. 'I'm sure you know your catechism very well indeed by now. Do you know, a little bird told me, that you are all very good girls, and know everything in the catechism. Is that true?'

Monica Blennerhasset smiles broadly and says, 'Yes, Father.' Some of the others nod.

'Now, I'm going to ask you something very hard, but very important. Can anyone recite the "Our Father"?'

We are taken aback, for a moment. The 'Our Father' isn't even in the catechism. But all hands shoot up, and some are waved about, eagerly. He asks Orla O'Connor, who had nodded to his first question. She says the prayer in a slow, considered voice, not the kind of tone we use for real catechism.

'Very good. The Lord's Prayer. It is a beautiful prayer, the Lord's Prayer. Jesus himself taught it to us. Jesus who loved little children, "Suffer the little children to come unto me," he said, didn't he?'

Nobody bothers to reply.

'Will you promise me something, girls?'

We nod.

'Will you promise me to say the Lord's Prayer every day for the rest of your lives?'

'Yes, Father,' we say, in our subdued voices, which probably sound pious to him.

'Very good. And now, since you are all such good girls, and know your catechism so well, I think you should have a half-day. What do you say, Miss O'Byrne?'

'Whatever you say, Father Harpur,' she says, her voice polite and respectful. She gives us a beaming smile, and we get up and file out. We knew we would get a half-day. The big girls told us about it. Miss O'Byrne warned the mothers, who are waiting, in the hall, under the statue of the Virgin.

'Well, how did you get on?' Mummy asks.

'Oh, all right,' I say. 'The priest was nice.' But I do not like the priest. I do not like him at all.

Instead of going home, we went to the Spring Show. It was my first time, and Ladies' Day. I recall it vividly. The hats. The free samples of flavoured milk and garlic sausage. The combine-harvesters. And the sound of the horses' feet, pounding, pounding, against the fragrant turf in the enclosure. It was a calm April day. Dull and poignant with the promise of summer. Like today.

51

6

BLOOD AND WATER

I have an aunt who is not the full shilling. 'The Mad Aunt' was how my sister and I referred to her when we were children, but that was just a euphemism, designed to shelter us from the truth which we couldn't stomach: she was mentally retarded. Very mildly so: perhaps she was just a slow learner. She survived very successfully as a lone farm woman, letting land, keeping a cow and a few hens and ducks, listening to the local gossip from the neighbours who were kind enough to drop in regularly in the evenings. Quite a few of them were: her house was a popular place for callers, and perhaps that was the secret of her survival. She did not participate in the neighbours' conversation to any extent, however. She was articulate only on a very concrete level, and all abstract topics were beyond her.

Had she been born in the fifties or sixties, my aunt would have been scientifically labelled, given special treatment at a special school, taught special skills and eventually employed in a special workshop to carry out a special job, certainly a much duller job than the one she pursued in reality. Luckily for her she was born in 1925 and had been reared as a normal child. Her family had failed to recognize that she was different from others and had not sought medical attention for her. She had merely been considered 'delicate'. The term 'mentally retarded' would have been meaningless in those days, anyway, in the part of Donegal where she and my mother originated, where Irish was the common, if not the only, language. As she grew up, it must have been silently conceded that she was a little odd. But people seemed to have no difficulty in suppressing this fact, and they judged my aunt by the standards which they applied to humanity at large: sometimes lenient and sometimes not.

She lived in a farmhouse in Ballytra on Inishowen, and once a year we visited her. Our annual holiday was spent under her roof. And had it not been for the lodging she provided, we could not have afforded to get away at all. But we did not consider this aspect of the affair.

On the first Saturday of August we always set out, laden with clothes in cardboard boxes and groceries from the cheap city shops, from the street markets: enough to see us through the fortnight. The journey north lasted nearly twelve hours in our ancient battered cars: a Morris Eight, dark green with fragrant leather seats, and a Ford Anglia are two of the models I remember from a long series of fourth-hand crocks. Sometimes they broke down en route and caused us long delays in nauseating garages, where I stood around with my father, while the mechanic tinkered, or went, with my sister and mother, for walks down country lanes, or along the wide melancholy streets of small market towns.

Apart from such occasional hitches, however, the trips were delightful odysseys through various flavours of Ireland: the dusty rich flatlands outside Dublin, the drumlins of Monaghan with their hint of secrets and better things to come, the luxuriant slopes, rushing rivers and expensive villas of Tyrone, and finally, the ultimate reward, the furze and heather, the dog-roses, the fuchsia, of Donegal.

Donegal was different in those days. Different from what it is now, different then from the eastern urban parts of Ireland. It was rural in a thorough, elemental way. People were old-fashioned in their dress and manners, even in their physiques: weather-beaten faces were highlighted by black or grey suits, shiny with age; broad hips stretched the cotton of navy-blue, flower-sprigged overalls, a kind of uniform for country women which their city sisters had long eschewed, if they ever had it. Residences were thatched cottages ... 'the Irish peasant house' ... or spare grey farmhouses. There was only a single bungalow in the parish where my aunt lived, an area which is now littered with them.

All these things accentuated the rusticity of the place, its strangeness, its uniqueness.

My aunt's house was of the slated, two-storey variety, and it stood, surrounded by a seemingly arbitrary selection of outhouses, in a large yard called 'the street'. Usually we turned into this street at about nine o'clock at night, having been on the road all day. My aunt would be waiting for us, leaning over the half-door. Even though she was deaf, she would have heard the car while it was still a few hundred yards away, chugging along the dirt lane: it was always that kind of car. She would stand up as soon as we appeared, and twist her hands shyly, until we emerged from the car. Then she would walk slowly over to us, and shake hands carefully with each of us in turn, starting with my mother. Care, formality: these were characteristics which were most obvious in her. Slowness.

Greetings over, we would troop into the house, under a low portal apparently designed for a smaller race of people. Then we would sit in front of the hot fire, and my mother would talk, in a loud cheery voice, telling my aunt the news from Dublin and asking for local gossip. My aunt would sometimes try to reply, more often not. After five minutes or so of this, she would indicate, a bit resentfully, that she had expected us earlier, that she had been listening for the car for over two days. And my mother, still, at this early stage of the holiday, in a diplomatic mood, would explain patiently, slowly, loudly, that no, we had been due today. We always came on the first Saturday, didn't we? John only got off on the Friday, sure. But somehow my mother would never have written to my aunt to let her know when we were coming. It was not owing to the fact that the latter was illiterate that she didn't write. Any neighbour would have read a letter for her. It was, rather, the result of a strange convention which my parents, especially my mother, always adhered to: they never wrote to anyone, about anything, except one subject. Death.

While this courteous ritual of fireside conversation was being enacted by my parents (although in fact my father never bothered to say anything), my sister and I would sit silently on our hard-backed chairs, fidgeting and looking at the familiar objects in the room: the Sacred Heart, the Little Flower, the calendar from Bells of Buncrana depicting a blond laughing child, the red arc for layers mash. We answered promptly, monosyllabically, the few questions my aunt put to us, all concerning school. Subdued by the immense boredoms of the day, we tolerated further boredom.

After a long time, my mother would get up, stretch, and prepare a meal of rashers and sausages, from Russells of Camden Street. To this my aunt would add a few provisions she had laid in for us: eggs, butter she had churned herself, and soda bread which she baked in a pot oven, in enormous golden balls. I always refused to eat this bread, because I found the taste repellent and because I didn't think my aunt washed her hands properly. My sister, however, ate no other kind of bread while we were on holiday at that house, and I used to tease her about it, trying to force her to see my point of view. She never did.

After tea, although by that time it was usually late, we would run outside and play. We would visit each of the outhouses in turn, hoping to see an owl in the barn, and then we'd run across the road to a stream which flowed behind the back garden. There was a stone bridge over the stream and on our first night we invariably played the same game: we threw sticks into the stream at one side of the bridge, and then ran as fast as we could to the other side in order to catch them as they sailed out. This activity, undertaken at night in the shadow of the black hills, had a magical effect: it plummetted me headlong into the atmosphere of the holidays. At that stream, on that first night, I would suddenly discover within myself a feeling of happiness and freedom that I was normally unaware I possessed. It seemed to emerge from some hidden part of me, like the sticks emerging from underneath the bridge, and it counteracted the faint claustrophobia, the nervousness, which I always had initially in my aunt's house.

Refreshed and elated, we would go to bed in unlit upstairs rooms. These bedrooms were panelled in wood which had been white once, but had faded to the colour of butter, and they had windows less than two feet square which had to be propped up with a stick if you wanted them to remain open: the windows were so small, my mother liked to tell us, because they had been made at a time when there was a tax on glass. I wondered about this: the doors were tiny, too.

When I woke up in the morning, I would lie and count the boards on the ceiling, and then the knots on the boards, until eventually a clattering of footsteps on the uncarpeted stairs and a banging about of pots and pans would announce that my mother was up and that breakfast would soon be available. I would run downstairs to the scullery, which served as a bathroom, and wash. The basin stood on a deal table, the water was in a white enamel bucket on the dresser. A piece of soap was stuck to a saucer on the window-sill, in front of the basin; through the window, you could see a bit of an elm tree, and a purple hill, as you washed.

In a way it was pleasant, but on the whole it worried me, washing in that place. It was so public. There was a constant danger that someone would rush in, and find you there, half undressed, scrubbing your armpits. I liked my ablutions to be private and unobserved.

The scullery worried me for another reason. On its wall, just beside the dresser, was a big splodge of a dirty yellow substance, unlike anything I had ever encountered. I took it to be some sort of fungus. God knows why, since the house was unusually clean. This thing so repelled me that I never even dared to ask what it was, and simply did my very best to avoid looking at it while I was in its vicinity, washing or bringing back the bucket of water from the well, or doing anything else. Years later, when I was taking a course in ethnology at the university, I realized that the stuff was nothing other than butter, daubed on the wall after every churning, for luck. But to me it symbolized something quite other than good fortune, something unthinkably horrible.

After dressing, breakfast. Rashers and sausages again, fried over the fire by my mother, who did all the cooking while we were on holiday. For that fortnight my aunt, usually a skilful frier of rashers, baker of bread, abdicated domestic responsibility to her, and adopted the role of child in her own house, like a displaced rural mother-in-law. She spent her time fiddling around in the henhouse, feeding the cat, or more often she simply sat, like a man, and stared out of the window while my mother worked. After about three days of this, my mother would grow resentful, would begin to mutter, gently but persistently, 'it's no holiday!' And my sister and I, even though we understood the reasons for our aunt's behaviour, as, indeed, did our mother, would nod in agreement. Because we had to share in the housework. We set the table, we did the washing up in an enamel basin, and I had personal responsibility for going to the well to draw water. For this, my sister envied me. She imagined it to be a privileged task, much more fun than sweeping or making beds. And of course it was more exotic than these chores, for the first day or so, which was why I insisted on doing it. But soon enough the novelty palled, and it was really hard work, and boring. Water is heavy, and we seemed to require a great deal of it.

Unlike our mother, we spent much time away from the kitchen, my sister and I. Most of every morning we passed on the beach. There was an old boathouse there, its roof almost caved in, in which no boat had been kept for many many years. It had a stale smell, faintly disgusting, as if animals, or worse, had used it as a lavatory at some stage in the past. Even though the odour dismayed us, and even though the beach was always quite deserted, we liked to undress in private, both of us together, and therefore going to great lengths with towels to conceal our bodies from one another, until such a time as we should emerge from the yawning door of the building, and run down the golden quartz slip into the sea.

Lough Swilly. Also known as 'The Lake of Shadows', my sister often informed me, this being the type of fact of which she was very fond. One of the only two fjords in Ireland, she might also add. That meant nothing to me, its being a fjord, and as for shadows, I was quite unaware of them. What I remember most about that water is its crystal clarity. It was greenish, to look at it from a slight distance. Or, if you looked at it from my aunt's house, on a fine day, it was a brilliant turquoise colour, it looked like a great jewel, set in the hills. But when you were in that water, bathing, it was as clear as glass: I would swim along with my face just below the lapping surface, and I would open my eyes and look right down to the sandy floor, at the occasional starfish, the tiny crabs that scuttled there, at the shoals of minnows that scudded from place to place, guided by some mysterious mob instinct. I always stayed in for ages, even on the coldest days, even when rain was falling in soft curtains around the rocks. It had a definite benign quality, that water. And I always emerged from it cleansed in both body and soul. When I remember it now, I can understand why rivers are sometimes believed to be holy. Lough Swilly was, for me, a blessed water.

The afternoons we spent *en famille,* going on trips in the car to view distant wonders, Portsalon or the Downings. And the evenings we would spend 'raking', dropping in on our innumerable friends and drinking tea and playing with them.

This pattern continued for the entire holiday, with two exceptions: on one Sunday we would go on a pilgrimage to Doon Well, and on one weekday we would go to Derry, thirty miles away, to shop.

Doon Well was my aunt's treat. It was the one occasion, apart from Mass, on which she accompanied us on a drive, even though we all realized that she would have liked to be with us every day. But the only outing she insisted upon was Doon Well. She would begin to hint about it gently soon after we arrived. 'The Gallaghers were at Doon Well on Sunday,' she might say. 'Not a great crowd at it!' Then on Sunday she would not change her clothes after Mass, but would don a special elegant apron, and perform the morning tasks in a particular and ladylike way: tiptoe into the byre, flutter at the hens.

At two we would set out, and she would sit with me and my sister in the back of the car. My sense of mortification, at being seen in public with my aunt, was mixed with another shame, that of ostentatious religious practices. I couldn't bear processions, missions, concelebrated masses: display. At heart, I was Protestant, and indeed it would have suited me, in more ways than one, to belong to that faith. But I didn't. So I was going to Doon Well, with my aunt and my unctuous parents, and my embarrassed sister.

You could spot the well from quite a distance: it was dressed. In rags. A large assembly of sticks, to which brightly coloured scraps of cloth were tied, advertised its presence and lent it a somewhat flippant, pagan air. But it was not flippant, it was all too serious. As soon as we left the safety of the car, we had to remove our shoes. The pain! Not only of going barefoot on the stony ground, but of having to witness feet, adult feet, our parents' and our aunt's, so shamelessly revealed to the world. Like all adults they had horrible feet, big and yellow, horny with corns and ingrown toenails, twisted and tortured by years of ill-fitting boots, no boots at all. To crown it, both my mother and aunt had varicose veins, purple knots bulging hideously through the yellow skin. As humiliated as anyone could be, and as we were meant to be, no doubt, we had to circle the well some specified number of times, probably three, and we had to say the Rosary, out loud, in the open air. And then my mother had a long litany to Colmcille, to which we had to listen and respond, in about a thousand agonies of shame, 'Pray for us!' The only tolerable part of the expedition occurred immediately after this, when we bought souvenirs at a stall, with a gay striped awning more appropriate to Bray or Bundoran than to this grim place. There we stood and scrutinized the wares on display: beads, statuettes, medals, snowstorms. Reverting to our consumerist role, we . . . do I mean I? I assume my sister felt the same about it all . . . felt almost content, for a few minutes, and we always selected the same souvenirs, namely snowstorms. I have one still: it has a painted blue backdrop, now peeling a little, and figures of elves and mushrooms under the glass, and, painted in black letters on its wooden base, 'I have prayed for you at Doon Well.' I bought that as a present for my best friend, Ann Byrne, but when I returned to Dublin I hadn't the courage to give it to her so it stayed in my bedroom for years, until I moved to Germany to study, and then I brought it with me.

We went to Derry without my aunt. We shopped and ate sausages and beans for lunch, in Woolworths. I enjoyed the trip to Derry. It was the highlight of the holiday, for me.

At the end of the fortnight, we would shake hands with my aunt in the street, and say goodbye. On these occasions her face would grow long and sad, she would always, at the moment when we climbed into the car, actually cry quietly to herself. My mother would say: 'Sure, we won't feel it now till it's Christmas! And then the summer will be here in no time at all!' And this would make everything much more poignant for my aunt, for me, for everyone. I would squirm on the seat, and, although I often wanted to cry myself, not because I was leaving my aunt but because I didn't want to give up the countryside, and the stream, and the clean clear water, I wouldn't think of my own unhappiness, but instead divert all my energy into despising my aunt for breaking yet another taboo: grown-ups do not cry.

My sister was tolerant. She'd laugh kindly as we turned out of the street onto the lane. 'Poor old Annie!' she'd say. But I couldn't laugh, I couldn't forgive her at all, for crying, for being herself, for not being the full shilling.

There was one simple reason for my hatred, so simple that I

understood it myself, even when I was eight or nine years old. I resembled my aunt physically. 'You're the image of your Aunt Annie!' people, relations, would beam at me as soon as I met them, in the valley. Now I know, looking at photos of her, looking in the glass, that this was not such a very bad thing. She had a reasonable enough face, as faces go. But I could not see this when I was a child, much less when a teenager. All I knew then was that she looked wrong. For one thing, she had straight unpermed hair, cut short across the nape of the neck, unlike the hair of any woman I knew then (but quite like mine as it is today). For another, she had thick unplucked eyebrows, and no lipstick or powder, even on Sunday, even for Doon Well, although at that time it was unacceptable to be unmade-up, it was outrageous to wear straight hair and laced shoes. Even in a place which was decidedly old-fashioned, she looked uniquely outmoded. She looked, to my city-conditioned eyes, like a freak. So when people would say to me, 'God, aren't you the image of your auntie!' I would cringe and wrinkle up in horror. Unable to change my own face, and unable to see that it resembled hers in the slightest . . . and how does a face that is ten resemble one that is fifty?. . . I grew to hate my physique. And I transferred that hatred, easily and inevitably, to my aunt.

When I was eleven, and almost finished with family holidays, I visited Ballytra alone, not to stay with my aunt but to attend an Irish college which had just been established in that district. I did not stay with any of my many relatives, on purpose: I wanted to steer clear of all unecessary contact with my past, and lived with a family I had never seen before.

Even though I loved the rigorous jolly ambiance of the college, it posed problems for me. On the one hand, I was the child of one of the natives of the parish, I was almost a native myself. On the other hand, I was what was known there as a 'scholar', one of the kids from Dublin or Derry who descended on Ballytra like a shower of fireworks in July, who acted as if they owned the place, who more or less shunned the native population.

If I'd wanted to, it would have been very difficult for me to steer a median course between my part as a 'scholar' and my other role, as a cousin of the little native 'culchies' who, if they had been my play-mates in former years, were now too shabby, too rustic, too outlandish, to tempt me at all. In the event, I made no effort to play to both factions: I managed by ignoring my relations entirely, and throwing myself into the more appealing life of the 'scholar'. My relations, I might add, seemed not to notice this, or care, if they did, and no doubt they were as bound by their own snobberies and conventions as I was by mine.

When the weather was suitable, that is, when it did not rain heavily, afternoons were spent on the beach, the same beach upon which my sister and I had always played. Those who wanted to swim walked there, from the school, in a long straggling crocodile. I loved to swim and never missed an opportunity to go to the shore.

The snag about this was that it meant passing by my aunt's house, which was on the road down to the lough: we had to pass through her street to get there. For the first week, she didn't bother me, prob-ably assuming that I would drop in soon. But, even though my mother had warned me to pay an early visit and had given me a head-scarf to give her, I procrastinated. So after a week had gone by she began to lie in wait for me: she began to sit on her stone seat, in front of the door, and to look at me dolefully as I passed. And I would give a little casual nod, such as I did to everyone I met, and pass on.

One afternoon, the teacher who supervised the group was walking beside me and some of my friends, much to my pride and discomfi-ture. When we came to the street, she called, softly, as I passed, 'Mary, Mary.' I nodded and continued on my way. The teacher gave me a funny look and said: 'Is she talking to you, Mary? Does she want to talk to you?' 'I don't know her,' I said, melting in shame. 'Who is she?' 'Annie, that's Annie Bonner.' He didn't let on to know anything more about it, but I bet he did: everyone who had spent more than a day in Ballytra knew everything there was to know about it, everyone, that is, who wasn't as egocentric as the 'scholars'.

My aunt is still alive, but I haven't seen her in many years. I never go to Inishowen now. I don't like it since it became modern and lit-tered with bungalows. Instead I go to Barcelona with my husband, who is a native Catalonian. He teaches Spanish here, part-time, at the university, and runs a school for Spanish students in Ireland during the summers. I help him in the tedious search for digs for all of them, and really we don't have much time to holiday at all.

My aunt is not altogether well. She had a heart attack just before Christmas and had to have a major operation at the Donegal Regional. I meant to pay her a visit, but never got around to it. Then, just before she was discharged, I learned that she was going home for Christmas. Home? To her own empty house, on the lane down to the lough? I was, to my surprise, horrified. God knows why, I've seen people in direr straits. But something gave. I phoned my mother and wondered angrily why she wouldn't have her, just for a few weeks. But my mother is getting on, she has arthritis, she can hardly walk herself. So I said, 'All right, she can come here!' But Julio was unenthusiastic. Christmas is the only time of the year he manages to relax: in January, the bookings start, the planning, the endless meetings and telephone calls. Besides, he was expecting a guest from home: his sister, Montserrat, who is tiny and dark and lively as a sparrow. The children adore her. In the end, my sister, unmarried and a lecturer in Latin at Trinity, went to stay for a few weeks in Ballytra until my aunt was better. She has very flexible holidays, my sister, and no real ties.

I was relieved, after all, not to have Aunt Annie in my home. What would my prim suburban neighbours have thought? How would Julio, who has rather aristocratic blood, have coped? I am still ashamed, you see, of my aunt. I am still ashamed of myself. Perhaps, I suspect, I do resemble her, and not just facially. Perhaps there is some mental likeness too. Are my wide education, my brilliant husband, my posh accent, just attempts at camouflage? Am I really all that bright? Sometimes, as I sit and read in my glass-fronted bungalow, looking out over the clear sheet of the Irish Sea, and try to learn something, the grammar of some foreign language, the names of Hittite gods, something like that, I find the facts running away from me, like sticks escaping downstream on the current. And more often than that, much more often, I feel in my mind a splodge of something that won't allow any knowledge to sink in. A block of some terrible substance, soft and thick and opaque. Like butter.

7

A VISIT TO NEWGRANGE

Mutti wrote to Erich. She would like to visit him in May. It had been two years since his last holiday in Bad Schwarzstadt and she was missing him. Besides, she was longing to see Ireland. A poster in the village travel agency depicted a scene in Connemara: a lake and hills and a donkey. The hills were so very green, she could hardly wait to climb them. And the sky was so very blue. And the donkey, so very friendly. It confirmed for her what she had always known, in her heart, about Ireland. She would arrive at 1.23 p.m. on the fourteenth, flight E4327. Perhaps Erich could spare a few hours from his studies to come and meet her? She realized that he was very busy and if he couldn't manage it, why, she wouldn't mind. She was used to travelling alone now, ever since Vatti died (fifteen years previously). It was true that she was sixty-eight and suffered from severe arthritis of the hip. But she could get along very well on her own. Her English, at least, was rather good. That much she had to admit. She'd been taking lessons all winter, at the Bad Schwarzstadt Adult Education Centre. Of course, she'd never been to an English-speaking country before. Not since before the War, anyway, when she had stayed with a family in Devon, improving her command of the language. The father had been a doctor. He had died on D-Day, tending the wounded on a French beach.

She had written a long letter, apparently. I didn't see it myself. Erich relayed its contents to me, in a light, satirical tone he sometimes uses for comic effect. Probably he embroidered the details as he went along: he has a wonderful imagination.

Underneath his soft chuckles, however, lay a core of hysteria so blatant that I knew I was meant to take heed of it. Fear, I supposed

it must be. Of Mutti. She was a little domineering, he had mentioned, once or twice? Oh, yes, indeed. With knobs on (Erich, like
many speakers of English as a foreign language, possesses a rich store
of colloquial expressions, and cannot resist employing them whenever possible). She was a real old battle-axe. Hard as nails. More
demanding than a two-year-old Ayatollah. More conservative than
Maggie Thatcher. A dyed-in-the-wool Lutheran. More puritanical
than John Knox.

I would have to move out.

It was only temporary.

She didn't realize he was living with me and the shock would be
too much for her. Her only son. It was only for two weeks. Why
make an issue of it? For a mere fortnight.

What about my mother? I politely enquired. She was dyed-in-
the-wool Catholic, more conservative than John Paul the Second,
more puritanical than the archbishop of Dublin. She'd had to turn a
blind eye on the fact that her daughter, her favourite daughter, her
fifth daughter, was living in a state of mortal sin. She'd had to accept
that life was different in Germany, different in Ranelagh, and soon
would be different in Tuam, County Galway. And what about me,
for heaven's sake? I was a dyed-in-the-wool Catholic, too, when you
came to think about it. Not just dyed, blued. Blued in the delicate,
gauzy wool of the Virgin Mary's cloak: her blue-white, whiter-than-
ordinary-white, artistically-draped, archetypal emblem of purity. A
Child of Mary, that's what I actually was, called to her service in the
chapel of Loreto on the Green when already a nubile impression-
able fifteen-year-old. What about that? And what about integrity,
courage and honesty, qualities which Erich claimed to prize above
all others?

Mutti was sixty-eight. She had severe arthritis of the hip. It was
only for two weeks. For heaven's sake.

On the thirteenth of May, I moved in with Jacinta who lives
around the corner. On the fifteenth, Erich invited me up for a cup
of tea, and I was introduced to Mutti.

She moved swiftly towards me, hobbling a little on the hip, and
encircled me in a warm embrace. I don't hug people's mothers, or
touch them at all if I can avoid it, and I was put off guard. Oblivious
of my confusion, she smiled radiantly, and effused:

'It is so nice to see you! Erich tells me all about you this morning. Such a nice surprise for me! I did not know Erich has a girlfriend, you see. In Ireland, that is!'

I shook her hand gently: slight, bony and hot, two rocky protrusions on its third finger bit into my palm. I held on for a second, and examined Mutti. She was about five feet tall and fragile, with bountiful curly grey hair, large gentian eyes, innumerable glittering teeth. A bygone beauty. 'Bygone' in my estimation, that is, although probably not in her own, if my experience of her type is anything to go on.

'Now, we have a nice cup of tea!'

She had motioned me towards the sofa, a handsome tweed one which I had bought the winter before in Kilkenny Design. We sat down, and Erich put on the kettle. Just a cup of tea. They'd had dinner in town, he explained. Yes, yes, acquiesced Mutti, such an excellent meal. I had not had dinner in town. I'd had nothing since lunch, and then I'd had two crispbreads and a slice of cheese.

I glared at Erich behind her back and he lilted: 'Perhaps you'd like a sandwich? Are you hungry?' 'Oh not at all,' I replied icily. 'Don't go to any trouble on my account.' My bitterness was wasted on him: he has weather-proof sensibilities, and can, at the flick of some interior zip, protect himself from all atmospheric variation. (This ability is one of the qualities which encouraged me to love him.) Blithely, he placed three mugs of tea, weak and tasteless, on the coffee table. We sipped it slowly, he and I marshalled up on the sofa opposite Mutti, who began her manoeuvres in oral English by requesting that I call her Friederika (I'd die first). Then she gave a full report of her trip from Germany and of the sightseeing tour she had taken that day. Questions of greater significance followed: Were my parents still alive? What did my father do for a living? What was my own occupation? Rank? Salary? Quick but efficient. The cross-examination over, we ceded to her command that we watch television, since this would aid her in her battle with the language. Before I left, it was arranged that I should collect both Mutti and Erich the following morning and drive them to Newgrange, which Erich considered an essential ingredient of any Irish tour worth its salt, as he put it himself. Mutti had clapped her hands at the suggestion.

'Oh, yes. That would be so nice! Newgrange. I think Herr Müller mentions it. Is it near Spiddal?'

A month prior to her visit, Mutti had borrowed a guide-book from the public library in Bad Schwarzstadt. The work of one Heinrich Müller, it was entitled *Ein kleines irisches Reisebuch*, and she had studied it with single-minded diligence until she knew its contents by heart. It was to be her inseparable vade-mecum during her holiday, and her main criterion for enjoyment in sightseeing was that the sight had been referred to by Herr Müller.

Therefore she had merrily and gratefully limped through the litter of O'Connell Street ('Oh! the widest street in Ireland!'), but the Powerscourt Centre had failed to arouse the mildest commendation. The Book of Kells had won her freshest laurels, but to the 'Treasures of Ireland' Exhibition, her reaction was one of chilled disappointment. 'Please, what is the meaning of the word "treasure"?' she had asked Erich, coming out of the museum onto Kildare Street. 'We did not have it in class, I believe.'

Herr Müller had spent the greater part of his *Reise* in Spiddal, and had devoted more than half his book, ten whole pages, to a graphic account of that settlement and its environs. Few corners of the western village were unfamiliar to Mutti, and she anticipated her sojourn there loudly and often and with the greatest of pleasure. Unfortunately, it would occur at the end of her stay in Dublin and last for no more than two days.

I arrived at the flat on the following morning, having taken a day's leave from my job in the Department of Finance.

'We'll go through the Phoenix Park,' I recommended brightly, determined to get value for my time. 'It's much more interesting that way, and only a bit longer. The President lives there. It's the biggest park in Europe.'

'Ah, yes,' responded Mutti noncommittally, as she settled into the passenger seat and opened a map. 'Can you show me where it is?'

I tried to lean across the brake and locate it for her, but Erich beat me to it, and, from the rear, indicated the relevant green patch. Mutti took a pencil from her handbag, held it poised in mid-air, and smiled: 'Are we going now?' On, James.

I drove to Charlemont Bridge.

'That's the canal,' I exclaimed brilliantly, waving at it as we turned off Ranelagh Road.

'Canal?'

'You know, Mutti. Canal. Not a river. Made by man. *Ein Kanal.*' Erich preferred the translation with caution:

Mutti had decreed that no German be spoken in her presence, since this might sabotage her chances of commanding the language.

'It's called the Grand Canal,' I continued, pedantically. 'There are two canals in Dublin, the Royal and the Grand. This is the Grand. It's quite a famous canal, actually. Poems have been written about it. Good poems. Quite well-known poems.'

Alas, it was not the leafy-with-love part of canal, it was the grotesque-with-graffiti bit, and Mutti stared, bemused, at peeling mildewed walls and disintegrating furry corpses. Even if it had been picturesque, I don't think its high-falutin' associations would have pulled any weight: Kavanagh had the misfortune to be post-Müller.

We drove towards Kilmainham in silence. The looming jail flooded my spirits with enthusiasm. The Struggle for Freedom was a favourite theme of Heinrich's, and Mutti, I had gathered from a few comments she had made, had also fallen victim to the romantic nostalgia for things Irish, historical, and bloody.

'Look!' I cried, 'there's Kilmain . . .'

But she had glimpsed the portico of the boys' school, which is impressive. And fake.

'Oh, Erich! How nice! Is it medieval, do you think?'

'Oh, yes, I think so, Mutti,' replied Erich, in his most learned voice. He knows nothing about Dublin, or architecture, or the Middle Ages.

'It looks like some of our German castles.'

'Look,' I pressed, 'that's Kilmainham Jail. The 1916 leaders were imprisoned there.' The light turned green. 'And shot,' I added, optimistically.

'In Bad Schwarzstadt we have two castles dating from the thirteenth century, Eileen, Marienschloss and Karlsschloss. They are so nice. People come to look from everywhere.'

'Really? I'd love to see them some day!'

The hint was ignored. I turned into the Park by the Islandbridge gate.

'This is the Phoenix Park,' the guided tour continued.

'Oh! A park. And we may drive in it. How nice.' Her tone was deeply disapproving. 'In Germany, we have many car-free zones. You know. Green zones, they are called. It is good without cars sometimes. For the health.'

At that moment, a Volkswagen sped around one of the vicious bends which are so common on the charming backroads of the Park. It took me unawares, and I was forced to swerve in order to avoid it. Swerve very slightly, and the Volkswagen was at fault.

'Oh, oh, oh, oh!' screamed Mutti, dapping her hands across her face. Through bony fingers her gentian eyes glared vindictively at me. I gritted my teeth and counted to fifty. Then I repeated fifty times 'a man's mouth often broke his nose', a proverb I had come across in *The Connaught Leader* a few weeks previously. Meanwhile, Mutti ignored the Pope's Cross, the lovely woods, the flocks of deer gambolling in the lovely woods, the American Embassy, the troops of travellers' ponies bouncing off the bonnet, the polo grounds and Áras an Uachtaráin.

'What town will we come to next?'

'Castleknock,' between one 'a man's mouth' and the next.

Scratch, scratch, went the pen on the map. Scratch scratch, through Blanchardstown, Mulhuddart, Dunshaughlin, Trim, past a countryside resplendent with frilly hedgerows, full-cream buttercups, fairy queen hawthorn, and, flouncing about everywhere, iridescent, giggling, fresh-from-Paris foliage. The sort of surrounding which sent many a medieval Irish monk into reams of ecstatic alliteration, as I liked to point out to my friends at this time of year, delicately reminding them that, even though I was a faceless civil servant, I had, in my day, sipped at the fountain of the best and most Celtic bards (taking a BA in Old Irish). Today I could practically smell the watercress and hazel. I could have taped the blackbird's song on my cassette. But I did not bother to emphasize the true Gaelic nature of the scenery for Mutti; tactfully leaving her to her own pedantic pursuits. Scritch scratch.

In County Meath we stopped for lunch. 'Ah,' gasped Mutti appreciatively, outside the 'olde worlde' hotel, 'this looks nice!' She guessed that an establishment with such a picturesque facade would have a high standard of cuisine. Alas, when we passed the promising threshold our eyes were greeted by a sign stating: 'lunch served in the bar', and our nostrils assailed by the ripe seedy odours of grease and alcohol. In Mutti's refined Lutheran opinion, drink was unspeakably Non-U, and her perfect nose wrinkled in disgust.

'Would you like something to drink, Mutti,' Erich asked, ordering two pints of Harp with great alacrity.

'Harp? What is that? Lemonade? Juice?'

'Well, no, it's a kind of light beer.'

'Juice. I will have some Harp juice, please. I am very thirsty.'

When the three drinks arrived, gleaming yellow and foaming over the edges, Mutti first clamped her lips together, then began to sip energetically. Service of the meal was slow, and she tapped her foot impatiently on the carpet.

'It is lucky I am not hungry. They are killing that pig for me, I think.'

In twenty minutes, the waitress arrived, bearing a dinner plate for Mutti, covered with slivers of pork and side dishes of carrots and cauliflower and cabbage and potatoes and gravy. She accepted generous helpings of everything . . . 'I am not hungry but I pay' . . . and, having dispensed with most of it, slid the leavings into a plastic bag which appeared, as if by magic, from her coat pocket:

'After all, we pay,' she said, not bothering to whisper. 'I eat this for lunch tomorrow. A little meat, that is all I need, now that I am older. I have a small appetite.'

Erich and I finished our salads hastily, and we proceeded to Newgrange.

It does not disappoint. Me. There are many among my acquaintance who hate it. They prefer Knowth and Dowth. Goethe. Shabby Victoriana. Woodworm. I relish the lambent, urbane face of immortality: Newgrange, pretentious crystal palace, lording it over the fat cowlands, the meandering fishbeds, reflecting the glory of the sun without a shadow of suburban modesty.

Erich, although he pays lip-service to its archaeological significance, belongs to the group of those who feel uneasy with this example of prehistoric P.R.; he senses that it is in dubious taste. I would not have been surprised to find Mutti of like mind. But no:

'It is very nice,' she gasped, to Erich, as we climbed the hill to the tumulus.

'I knew you'd like it, Mutti,' he simpered, his eyes rivetted to the figure of the guide, a slender and provocative one, neatly glazed in luminous yellow pants and white T-shirt. She posed on a standing stone outside the mound and outlined its history in a few well-chosen words, then led the creeping party of tourists along the narrow passage to the burial chamber. Mutti had been pleased by the outside of the grave, but she was in raptures within. The ice-cold room at the centre of the hill enchanted her soul, and she oohed and ahed so convincingly that the lemon-clad one directed her remarks expressly at her, catching her large eyes and ignoring the other, less charming, members of the little group. When her spiel was over and she made the mandatory request for questions, only one was asked, and that by Mutti:

'Are there any runic stones here?' How silly, I thought. But, of course, there were. It was possible that one stone at the side of the vault contained writing. Had the guide invented this titbit to satisfy Mutti? Hardly. She had an honest, if tarty, face.

After the tour, Mutti and I lingered in the burial chamber. The others left, gradually, but she seemed to want to stay, and I felt it my duty to remain, too. What with her arthritis. Gradually, however, I realized that I was happy to be in the cool greyness of the place. It has, I noticed for the first time, a curious intimacy, the character of a kitchen, a space at the centre of the home where people gather to sustain themselves. To survive. And, although it is as chill as a tomb. . . . it is a tomb, after all . . . this room has a hearth, a focus: the guide had explained that once a year the sun would pour through the opening in the outer wall, stream along the entrance passage, and flood the chamber with light. Illumination for the immortal dead.

Mutti, tracing with her delicate fingers the spiralling patterns on the tombstones, turned to me:

'Imagine how nice it is here on December twenty-one. So very nice!'

Her eyes glowed with a candour they had not held before, and for the first time since our meeting we looked at each other full in the face. We laughed. Mutti moved towards me slowly, because of the hip, and I had an impulse to run and embrace her, to kiss her. She would not have been embarrassed, that was the sort of thing she did. But I do not kiss people's mothers, or touch anyone at all, if I can avoid it. So I hesitated.

Erich crept into the chamber. Mutti hobbled over to him and clasped his hand.

'It's time to go,' he said. 'Haven't you had enough of this creepy old mausoleum?'

So brief are our moments of salvation. So sudden. So easily lost.

8

NIGHT OF THE FOX

'What I like about it is seeing the light in the window when we arrive and then going into the kitchen and it's bright and hot and Nana's there and Granda's there and we get our tea.'

We're going to the country.

It's a long weekend. It's a long way to the country. We've made good headway, however, in spite of some hiccups (roadworks in Dorset Street: 'Dorset Street's not real!' somebody had told me earlier in the week, but I forgot that in the rush of getting away). In any case, we are out of town by six o'clock, out on the road to Wavesend, the North Road. Soon its clipped hedges and depressingly straight line have given way to a narrower winding way overhung with elms. The ditches are creamy with meadowsweet. Hawthorn blossoms drip like lazy snow on to the bonnet of the car.

'When will we get there? How many hours? Five hours? A hundred hours?'

We play 'What am I?' with the boys. Simon, who is almost seven, plays seriously: he is not too old for this kind of thing, or too young. He works indoors. He makes something, something you can eat. He enjoys his job. He is a baker. Timmy's mind is not the kind that focuses easily on games, on any kind of game, or on anything else for that matter. He works outdoors. He grows something. His job is fun. It turns out he's a robber.

'He's chea-ea-tin'.'

'I am not. I'm not cheatin', sure I'm not, Mammy!'

Erich turns up the cassette player and shouts at them over the roar of somebody's concerto. The car swerves slightly and I frown.

The thing is not to let them get at you. If you let them get at you you could crash the car. You would certainly get a headache.

Sooner than is wise we have to stop for food: Simon is so hungry, he can't last till we're even close to a halfway stage. I turn down an avenue to a place we've often used before for travellers' snacks; it is called 'The Traveller's Rest', like many pubs and cafés along the way. (One of our games, on one of our journeys, was counting them. After five we lost interest.) But unlike most of those establishments it is an old, comfortable hotel, set amidst rolling golf greens and overlooking a lake which might be artificial, might have been constructed a hundred years ago just to provide this elegant place with a view, but looks natural enough to fool us. We park in what I think is the usual place but something has happened: the hotel has disappeared. At least the house we know is no longer there. Instead there are some new buildings, faked to look old. They are half finished; piles of cement and machinery are lying about. We can't see anyone and we can't find anything that looks like an entrance.

'Maybe it's further up. Maybe we've parked in the wrong place!' I suggest. I am always ready to doubt my judgement, to believe myself wrong. Sometimes I am justified in this attitude, sometimes not. And now I realize as I walk that some of the features are familiar. Where the new terrace is, there used to be an old terrace, with a fancy balustrade and pink and white geraniums in stone pots. The new terrace has nothing, as yet, relieving its bareness. Indeed, like all the building, it has the dead wettish look of fresh concrete and its sour smell. Eventually we try a door that looks forbidding: I think it might be the way into a golf club, some private exclusive place that we, in our work- and school-weary clothes, with our tired unglamorous faces, have no right to enter.

As we approach the door we meet a stylishly dressed woman who stares past us: she has the unfriendly eyes of a fashion model or some pampered, oft-stared at personage. I expect to be repulsed. But once inside the door I have the feeling of being in a familiar place that has somehow changed beyond recognition. It is like a room I have visited in a previous existence, or have become familiar with from the pages of a book. Gradually, however, we realize that enormous alterations have been carried out on the hotel both inside and out, but that the basic ground plan, although enlarged, is the same as before. Thus the lobby is three times as big and ten times as elegant as it formerly was, but it is more or less in the same place as the old, comfortable lobby we used to drink coffee in.

Similarly, the bar is in the same quarters as the old bar: in fact, the bar itself, the wooden counter with a huge mirror behind, is exactly the same; it was good enough to endure the transition, apparently. Only the furniture and the interior decoration has been altered here, altered beyond recognition. Antique, or antique-look, sofas and easy chairs, no two doing anything as vulgar as matching, but all blending harmoniously together. Deep custom-designed carpets. The toilets are the most splendid of all, and we all comment on them.

'Of course you pay for all the elegance!'

'How much did it cost, Dad?'

Simon wants to know the cost of everything. It has become an obsession with him, one with which I have difficulty being patient. For once Erich gives him a civil answer.

'Ten pounds.'

'Ten pounds! Ten pounds! For two cups of coffee and two sand-wiches and two glasses of coke! Ten pounds! They weren't even big sandwiches, were they, Mum?'

'Not really,' I have to agree. They were small sandwiches. The coffee was not especially good, either; it was probably instant but it was so bad you couldn't tell whether it was or not. Normally I would forgive the faults and the expense in a place as luxurious and splendid as this has become. I like luxury and precious trappings, easy panache. Not this time. The refurbishing of 'The Traveller's Rest' has left me thoroughly disorientated. It was permeated with a sense of *déjà vu*, elusive feelings I couldn't get a grip on. It wasn't real.

We are going to visit my parents in their summer cottage on the northern coast. They bought this cottage five years ago, five years after my father retired. It was something they'd been planning to do for years, to return to the country, to live in the place, or near the place, where they had been born. But when the time came at long last they found they couldn't stick Wavesend all the year round. It is no longer the place it was when they were young, a place where families lived and worked and which was, purely incidentally, also a very picturesque, beautiful place. Now it is more of a quiet holiday resort and most of its houses are summer cottages. It's hard to live year round in a place like that. So they spend six months there and six months in the city in their old house on Exeter Place. Usually in Exeter Place they are ill, coughing and having headaches and flutterings of the heart. They are up and down to the doctor. On more than one occasion one of them has been in hospital, but so far they've always come out, recovered. Usually in Wavesend they are well. Fat and sunburned, they spend their days planting vegetables and cutting the lawn and going for walks on the beach and drinks in the local pub. It is a good life but not, my mother says, in winter. In winter you have to be in town.

We visit them two or three times each summer, usually during July and August when the children have their summer holidays. Now it is June and we are going because a cousin of ours from Wavesend, Manus, is ill. He is one of the permanent Wavesend people, and he has been a good friend to my mother and father during their retirement: he is the sort of man who will come and fix a burst pipe or mend the motor mower whenever necessary. In fact he comes to the house and cuts the grass for my parents when they are away in Dublin and his wife, Marie, lights a fire in the kitchen to keep the place aired. A few months ago he started forgetting things. The vet made an appointment to come and check his small dairy herd and it went clean out of his head. He promised Marie he would get her a packet of bayleaves when he was in town at a mart (he is a farmer) and came home without them. He forgot to pay the ESB bill and they were cut off suddenly to the great risk of their milk, settling in electrical cooling vats in the dairy. Other incidents like that occurred. Minor but accumulating. Then about three weeks ago he got a bad headache. A tumour was diagnosed. By now he is in a state of semiconsciousness. The tumour is inoperable. He has been given a few months.

The children, our children, do not, of course, know any of this. They know that Manus is sick but it means nothing to them. They hardly remember who Manus is, although I explain. Manus, the man who gives us the asparagus and the milk. Manus has been in the habit of bringing us gifts of unusual vegetables, artichokes, asparagus, egg plants, which he grows organically as a hobby. They are fresh and delicious, but Simon and Timmy have never eaten any of them. They don't eat any kind of vegetable except potato. Neither do they like the milk which Manus carries up to the house every evening. They turn up their noses when they see it frothing and foaming in the white enamel bucket. When they go to bed my mother pours it into bottles and puts them in the fridge. Next day she pretends she's bought them from the shop.

It is midnight by the time we reach Wavesend. When I turn down the lane that leads to my parents' house I see the lights on in their windows. And I see also two smaller yellow lights in their garden hedge. Lights that move, brilliant yellow, yellower than any light I know, against the black hedge. I see these lights, but nobody else does; the boys are half asleep, Erich is talking about Beethoven and Mozart. Simon is like Beethoven, he says. Timmy is like Mozart. I have no knowledge of music and no memory for it. Erich used to play games with me: Guess what this is? Who wrote it? What instruments are being used? He's given up on that. It's too late: when I was Simon's age I'd never heard the names Beethoven and Mozart, let alone any of their music. But I agree with him about the contrasting characters. I have picked up the basic biographical clichés.

'Look!'

Erich looks and does not see. Timmy sits up and leans against his window. Simon grumbles.

'Do you see?'

It is a fox, a small, perfect fox, imprisoned momentarily in the beam of the headlights. His brush stands firmly up, his little sharp face is cocked, looking at us with eyes that are not yellow anymore, but glittering ebony like ponds in moonlight.

'Look! Look, Simon, look!'

Already he has disappeared into the darkness. Nobody has seen him apart from me: the boys never do see wild animals; you have to be older than them, I think, or at least quieter, in order to catch sight of a fox or a hare or even a rabbit, which I see dozens of times as I drive along through the countryside. Both boys are sceptical and do not really believe that I have seen a fox. I can understand their scepticism, and their faint resentment. I wish Simon, at least, had caught a glimpse of it because he likes animals so much. In books, that is.

★ ★ ★

'He's not so well,' my father says in his shy diffident voice. His bushy old eyebrows meet in a puzzled frown as if he does not understand why this should be. Manus is less than half his age, one of the young men he depended upon.

'Ah well, you never know how things will go. He may improve.' Erich does not know Manus and the subject of illness is distasteful to him. He has been seriously ill himself in the not too distant past, not with Manus' illness but with another serious disease. He does not want the topic broached. Neither do I. 'I am always optimistic, you know!'

'Yes,' my father laughs his little apologetic but rather gleeful laugh. 'I heard Gorbachev saying something today, yez didn't hear it, did yez? It was very good like . . . what was it, something like "I see the glass half full and the people see it half empty." I thought it was good.'

Erich and I exchange a look.

'Yes,' says Erich, 'oh yes. I always see the glass half full, while Lennie here sees it half empty. If not completely empty. She is a pessimist, are you not?'

'I suppose so.' I am embarrassed when Erich teases me in the presence of my parents. I wish he wouldn't do it. They like it a bit, but no more than me, do not know how they are supposed to respond. My father, luckily, can always pretend not to hear anything he doesn't grasp fully since he is partially deaf.

My mother is running in and out of the scullery setting the table and making tea. As usual, we will have cheese and cold ham and bread and tea.

'We had dinner in a hotel on the way. It cost a hundred pounds,' Simon informs her in his loud voice. He is wide awake by now.

I try to correct this. Mother is capable of believing it, of believing that we would buy a dinner costing a hundred pounds on our way to the country and bring her as a gift a bunch of flowers purchased at a garage on the roadside and costing two pounds fifty: the only thing they had, the only thing I had time to get. Erich had got them, actually, along with another item I'd urgently required: a packet of sanitary towels. He'd said: 'I am not going to ask for them!' but I knew he would. He is like Mozart. When he came out, with the bunch of oldish carnations and the see-through plastic bag, he said, 'I had to say the words sanitary towels three times. The fellow in there had never heard of them.'

'Did you have to tell him about the facts of life as well?'

'He's at your window now; why don't you tell him yourself?'

The boy's face at the window, waiting to serve the petrol, was not red or ostensibly embarrassed, but bland, expressionless. So I knew he was either embarrassed or scornful, waiting for us to move on so that he could laugh at us with some companion. I quickly gave my order and money and got away.

My mother, in strong contrast to my father, is loquacious. She loves to talk, to transform the ordinary events of her life into stories. The gory details of illness, any illness, always provide her with excellent copy, and she tells us a great deal about Manus. More than we want to know. 'Poor Manus, there's nothing they can do for him in Luke's. The thing is growing so fast, it's really just taking over the whole brain now.' She uses her hand to demonstrate how it's growing. Her hand has grown puffy lately, and the sun has highlighted its veil of coffee-coloured spots. I glance at my own hand, large but as yet thin. The right hand is a comforting pasty white but the left is freckling, sure enough. I touch the black mole on the left side of my face, where something has begun to stiffen. The left is my dangerous side; I have always feared it. That is where the end will come first. Feeling the tinge of nausea which that touch and thought always stimulate, I quickly return my attention to my mother's tale. Her hand is still boldly illustrating the air above the table while her voice continues to provide supporting text. To hear her speak you would swear she had been inside Manus's head with the surgeons, peering at it with a magnifying glass, probing with the scalpel. I see a stalk of meadowsweet putting out more and more white fronds, each one foaming with a myriad tiny blossoms. 'In the end it'll start to bleed and then . . .'

She shakes her head fatalistically.

'We'll miss the milk,' she says.

'And the asparagus,' I acquiesce, observing Erich's expression of disgust. He hates the mercenary side of humanity, a side with which I am very familiar. My mother will, given half a chance, elaborate on Manus's financial affairs and the problems his widow may have to face. She will hint at the plight of the children: to do more than hint would be to go too far, at this stage, but we all get the message. And his imminent death is transformed from a personal tragedy to something akin to a devaluation of the pound or some kind of purely economic crisis. Manus, like a lot of married men, is more than just a human being. He is a breadwinner. Other humans depend on him for their sustenance: his loss will be greater than that of a man or woman with a smaller responsibility. Will it also, in some way, be less? I have my suspicions but I do not want to consider their implications right now, so I shy away from them.

We are going to see Manus on Saturday afternoon, but the morning is ours, for pleasure. First we go to the beach so that Simon and Timmy can play. It is Whit Saturday. My father tells us that when he was a child they were never allowed to go to the shore on Whit Sunday, because if you got a cut on that day it would never heal.

'Don't pay any attention to him!' my mother laughs. 'It's not Sunday anyway, is it? Go on down to the beach and let the boys enjoy themselves.'

The beach, according to my mother, is the most magnificent beach in Ireland. It's the longest and the finest, and moreover it's got some special award from the EC for being the most unpolluted. Possibly it is the best and biggest beach in Europe, possibly, for all I know, in the world. We trudge down to it, across the sandy field that separates it from the house. Lapwings take fright as we pass and wheel around our heads, frantically twittering 'Peewee, peewee!' 'They sound like a computer game,' observes Simon, and Erich and I smile, thinking that Simon is very clever. 'Peewee, peewee!' We arrive at the beach.

Two miles of white sand, reddish when it's rained as it has earlier this morning. A wide bay, shirred by shadows, into which the hills fall gracefully like smooth-haunched bathers. Behind the beach are dunes, giving way to a saucer-shaped valley. The lip of hills that shelters it is low but variegated, mysterious to look at. The most distant hills are black, those slightly nearer green. The closest of all are olive green, moss green, brown and silver. I look at the hills and the greyish-white sky while I kick ball with Simon, help Timmy build a sandcastle. Why don't they build themselves? I ask Erich. But he doesn't hear; he is walking along by the edge of the waves plugged into his walkman, listening to his eternal music and staring at the terns which dive into the sea at regular intervals with a shocking white splash. What does he hear when he listens? I would like to know but I never will. When I first knew him he didn't seem to care about music. Gradually it has become an obsession. I think this dates from the time of his illness, the time he had his heart operation. Four years ago, at the time of Timmy's birth. I was in Holles Street, having Timmy, while he was in another hospital, being cut to bits. We try to forget that time and to forget that Erich is always in danger, and mainly we succeed. As time passes we assume that danger lessens, although probably the opposite is the case. The operation has left its mark on Erich, however, in more ways than one. He knows something that I don't know, I suspect, and it is not something he can teach me. The names of concertos, the lives of the composers, he tries with those. But he can't give me the music.

I think of a piece of coral. There is no coral, naturally, on this northern strand. The rocks, however, which border it at one end are black and soft, lacy with clefts and multi-shaped fissures. You could guess that the Giant's Causeway is not too far away. In one part of the bay great arches have formed where the sea has bitten through the basalt. You can sit and watch oystercatchers and gulls flying under the arches as you listen to the waves crashing on the rocks. In spite of their grey and black colours, their texture reminds me of coral reefs in the south seas. Stones of pink and stones of white, growing and growing and growing.

After lunch we drive to the hospital. I am driving: I do not want to concede this power to my father or mother, who have offered to play chauffeur. I am afraid to let them drive me anywhere, afraid of where they will take me and how long I will have to stay. If I drive I will have the ultimate say in what we decide to do. My mother knows this and that is why she is looking disgruntled, climbing awkwardly into the back seat. My father sits beside me in the front. My mother, possibly to atone for feeling annoyed, is doling out peppermint sweets and the air is full of their aroma.

The meadowsweet froths out of the ditches like bubbles on the top of a bucket of new milk. Behind it the rhododendron bushes have gone out of control so that they are not bushes but trees, not shrubbery but forests, dangling their enormous flowers. Mostly purple, some the more brilliant exotic pink.

Erich is asleep. I can hear him snoring, a thin snore like a whistle. The hospital is on the outskirts of the town and has substantial grounds. The children are not allowed in to visit, we are told in the lobby. Erich is quick to offer his services as minder. 'Sure, Lennie can come down and let you up in a few minutes,' my mother, always ready to organize, says. 'I doubt if we'll have to stay long.'

I feel sick, hearing these words. They get me in the gut, not with sadness, but with something closer to either fear or nausea. What is it I am so afraid of?

We walk falteringly up the stairs (falteringly because my mother and father are old and each has one good hip and one bad, the good one made of plastic. They do not negotiate stairs easily, particularly stairs that are strange to them). The hospital is like all others I have been in, rather more spacious and comfortable than some. There are wide corridors with no beds in them, and equipment seems to be stored in its proper place, out of sight. The cutbacks you hear so much about don't seem to have taken effect here, not visibly anyway. A few nurses scuttle along. We find the ward Manus is in: Saint Joseph's. It is a big room containing about twenty beds. 'He's down near the far corner,' my mother whispers. Her voice is reverent; it is the voice she uses in church. 'You won't know him. Don't expect to know him, he looks so different. He's in that second last bed, I think, do you see there, near that table with the flowers on it?'

The flowers are sweet peas, I can see that much from here, but my mother cannot since she is not wearing her glasses. Neither can she see that the bed she has indicated is empty. I do not point this out to her, but walk slowly, measuring my step to hers and my father's, until they can see it for themselves.

'Hm, that's odd now,' my mother looks around. Her face wears a rather sharp and business-like look, an expression it gets when she is dealing with people whom she considers inferior to herself. A lot of people fall into this category, including me and my father.

A nurse comes and tells us. He's been moved. He's in Intensive care. We can't visit him.

My mother is not going to give up so easily.

'My daughter has come all the way from Dublin especially to see him. Especially. It may be her last chance.'

'You can look in at him, I suppose,' the nurse concedes. She is quite young but authoritative. She looks at me with an expression that is both sympathetic and scornful. My mother, I realize, must seem slightly eccentric to some younger people. The strong will, the independence, the pushiness which were powerful when she was younger herself have hardened into oddness, to be humoured if it's easier, not to be feared.

We follow the nurse to a lift and along a wider, much quieter corridor.

'There,' she says, and leaves us.

My mother peers through the window. My father, obedient as always, looks; his eyesight is not the best, he probably can't see anyway. I stand as far away as I can and fix my gaze on the curtains. They are a dusty pink, smoky pink I think it is called, and are made of imitation linen. I look closely at the little uneven cropped lines, the broken weave.

'Poor Manus,' my mother says, shrugging her shoulders. Shrugging him off. 'Doesn't he look dreadful?'

We nod.

The nurse comes and beckons us away. My mother, on the way out, questions her about Manus. But of course she gives us no solid information.

We all leave the hospital together and walk along the paved pathway to the carpark. The sky is still overcast but the sun is occasionally making an effort to break through. Now it pierces a bank of grey cloud and the slabs at our feet grow lighter, almost yellow, for a minute. Our shadows appear before us, faint diffident shadows. They move along slowly ahead like silent guides, each shadow blending into the next so that you cannot tell where one person's ends and the other's begins.

9

HOLIDAY IN THE LAND OF
MURDERED DREAMS

'Can I turn your sheets down, madam?' the loud voice of a bellboy bellowed through a partly opened door on the first floor of Finbar's Hotel. It surprised Detta that they still performed this antiquated ceremony, one with which she was perfectly familiar. The voice which replied to the bellboy sounded even more surprised than she was. Detta could not hear any actual words, but the tone resounded with shock, guilt and terrible disbelief – the unmistakable tone of one caught in flagrante something or other. Actually, the disembodied, frustrated voice might as well have shouted 'Here I am, committing adultery!' for all interested parties to hear. Poor fellow! (Because it was, of course, the man who dealt with the bellboy. Ultimately, women suffer most in adultery, but men get to deal with its most embarrassing crises. Would you ever take out the bins, love!) Detta glanced at her companion, Karl Brown – a complete stranger whom she had just met at the reception desk. The glaze of his blue eyes told her that he too recognized that panicky tone of voice, and understood precisely what it meant. He looked as if he understood, as well, the special quality of whatever illicit pleasure had been intercepted. He knew what the guilty couple had been *at*. A man who looked like Karl Brown would probably be a specialist on sex.

Detta was surprised by a stirring, a tricky little twitch of desire. She sneezed, as she always did when suddenly aroused.

'Stop!' Detta warned her body. 'Down! You've known this man for two minutes! For God's sake!'

Karl Brown smiled knowingly at her. In guilty silence, they

walked along the hotel corridor, which was not sexy at all. It looked like the inside of a pipe, or an artery in the human anatomy. It was like strolling through the alimentary canal.

'And you?' With a sigh he reverted to small talk. 'What do you do?'

'My job? I own a flower shop as a matter of fact.'

As a matter of fact.

'Tulips?'

'I sell other kinds as well. But yes. Tulips.'

'Tulips are the best flowers,' he said, in his chocolatey, musical voice, a voice designed to accompany unimaginable pleasures.

Detta felt their drooping damp thick petals, their turgid stems.

'Oh yes!' she replied, wondering if his burgundy velvet jacket, his snowy embroidered shirt, were a joke. He looked like a chocolate as well as sounding like one. 'They are.'

Actually her favourite flower was the narcissus. But who could ever admit to that?

The walk to room 105 was all too short. They reached it in seconds. Karl Brown looked at Detta. A question, bright as a cornflower, shone in his eyes – or did it?

She looked away.

Then he was gone, her Mozart chocolate, seductive as a sonata, gone before she could say 'Maybe a drink?'

Detta opened the door. The room spread before her, dim and seductive in pale mushroomy light. Its blue carpet was thick and soft, and its enormous bed, shaped like a medieval longship, beckoned lovers to its fluffy bosom. Try me! called the sirens of the bed.

Detta turned her back on it and walked to the window. She pulled back the heavy curtains. The room, facing north across the river, filled to the brim with clear pale light.

She smiled, kicked off her shoes, and then pulled off her other clothes: her stockings, suit, bra. Her skin sighed relief, as her body expanded to its natural size – fourteenish going on sixteenish – and resumed its real, loose, shape. She walked across to the bathroom, the soles of her feet relishing the thick woollen pile of the carpet: in her flat in Amsterdam the floors were all wooden.

After peeing, she gazed at herself in an enormous wall mirror.

'Not *too* bad!' she said, aloud, into the cool silveriness of the perfect little bath room. 'Considering!' What she saw was a short woman with a perky blonde bob, no waist to speak of, small hands and feet. Her bottom had ballooned to about twice as big as it was five years ago, and there were little brown moles and freckles and pimples in places which used to be snow white. She sighed and cradled her single breast, imagining, for a second, Karl's touch there. Her hand brushed a slab of shivering thigh. She sneezed again. A tiny disappointment stabbed the inside of her groin.

'This can't be happening!' She grabbed a fluffy white dressing gown from the back of the door and wrapped her treacherous body in it, knotting the belt viciously. 'Cop on, cop on!' Angrily, she dashed to the minibar, and snatched a tin of tonic and a minature bottle of gin from its well-stocked shelves. Sitting against the ballooning pillows in the prow of the bed, like the Lady of Shallot, she mixed her drink and swallowed half of it in one gulp.

Alcohol could take the edge off any attraction, as well as the opposite.

Relieved, she relaxed and surveyed the room.

Although warmer than necessary in temperature, it was cool in colour. In the pale evening sunshine it was translucent as the inside of an iceberg: many shades of white and pale blue; sudden glimmers of silver. Everything was blue now, it was the colour of the nineties. Even the Dublin gin gleamed like a luminous sapphire in its tiny bottle. They used to say blue was too cold for rooms. When Detta had last been in Finbar's Hotel, brown was the favourite colour. Chestnut carpets with swirly brown leaf patterns on them, gently muted by dust and sun. Fawn flocked wallpaper, embossed with elephantine roses, covered many of the rooms. There were variations, of course. Endless variations. Rooms had been redecorated by the old owners, the FitzSimons, according to necessity, not choice, so that by 1970, when Detta was last here, almost every room had evolved its own distinct character. They had numbers, but could just as easily have been given names. The Wine Room. The Room with the Piano. The Room of the Creaking Board. Mr O'Hanlon's Room.

Mr O'Hanlon's Room was the one she remembered. Was this it? She couldn't recall its number – if she had, she would have demanded it for the night. But all she remembered was that it was on the first floor. The memory is selective of details: correctly, deliberately so, she had read somewhere once. Or is it simply erratic? Some memories, the significance of which she could seldom fathom, remained firmly embedded in the consciousness, while others were shredded. Thus she remembered the creaking board very well – it was the sixth board from the door of room 203. And the wallpaper in the Green Room, which was white with a green sprig, lily of the valley, very pretty and feminine in a hotel which did not, on the whole, boast many feminine touches or even many women. (In those days, guests, and staff, in grade-two city hotels were mainly men. Probably the same was true of every other grade of hotel as well.) But she couldn't remember, at all, the colour of the corridors, or even of the dining room, although she retained an impression of its shape and contours. Was it wallpapered, like the bedrooms, or painted some 1960s colour? Magnolia? Mint green? The tables had been draped in white cloths, she remembered. But then almost all hotel tables had been, and still were, so recalling that was not much of a feat of memory. What kind of cutlery did they have? Gone. Crockery? Or delph as people called it? White with a gold rim? Willow pattern?

You're making it up, Detta! she said aloud again. You haven't a clue. It's all gone from your head and perhaps from everybody's head. Sunk, like the Titanic, into the bottomless ocean of the forgotten past. Mental waste. How much of it the minds of the human race has generated, millions of tons of forgotten facts, dumped at the bottom of the ocean, crushed or shredded or melted.

Gone. And in physical fact the Finbar's Hotel Detta once knew was now archaeology. The place had been renovated over and over again, and practically rebuilt anew just a year ago by these new owners, as, no doubt, generations of houses on this site had been built and demolished, built and demolished, over the centuries. The lives of layer upon layer of humanity lay under the edifice now called 'Finbar's Hotel'. Forgotten, half-forgotten, but inescapably there, inescapably *here*, making their mark, ever since the Vikings first erected some wooden turf-topped hut in the place whenever they came here. The founders of Dublin. Where's my Carlsberg? What a bunch!

Detta felt her head begin to protest. She swallowed her drink and poured herself another. The pressures of the present, and of her personal history, were all she could deal with at the moment: she couldn't cope with the Vikings, and all that went before and came after, just now.

Brown, the chocolate American, popped back into her mind momentarily. She pushed him out again, almost laughing aloud at herself, at the pointlessness of her desire. The sort of love her body still yearned for was firmly consigned to her past. You'd think it would know that! What interested her anyway, now, were other forms of love, less physical but not less intense. She was still learning them. Even if she'd had confidence in her body, she wouldn't want to muddle up her new kinds of love with the old, messy kind, the kind she had been such a mistress of once, in a life – and a body – that seemed as foreign to her now as if it had belonged to someone else.

She glanced at her watch. It was only six thirty. She should eat something before the meeting. But there was plenty of time. Stretching her limbs, she luxuriated in the springy newness of the snow-white duvet; she allotted herself another half-hour's day-dreaming.

The owners of the hotel were Dutch. She hadn't known that until the receptionist downstairs had told her. Coincidence? Not so much of a coincidence, really, as it would have once been. Dublin was becoming more cosmopolitan by the minute. Or more European, rather. Its relationship with the rest of the world seemed tenuous. Irish people still seemed to believe that Europe was the whole world, the only world they had to conquer. America was a sort of laughable rich relation, benign but too familiar to be taken seriously. You couldn't imagine anyone in Ireland apart from a few right-wing politicians aiming to be more American, whereas becoming more European (as well as aiming to loot Europe, while giving as little as possible in return) had been the national pious aspiration for decades. And the rest of the world was still just the rest of the world. Irrelevant.

Detta found herself writing a letter to the paper, or a short arti-cle, as her mind wandered over this topic, generalizing wildly about the Irish and the Dutch and the rest of them. A column, that's what she'd like to write about it. She realized that she had been writing columns in her head since she boarded the plane, since she started thinking in English again. In Dutch she tended to think about business, what she had to order, who she had to pay. She thought about buying flowers and potatoes, about which friend's birthday was coming next and what would be a suitable present. Her language was the language of work and domesticity, as her life was. In Dutch she was a stereotypical Dutchwoman, practical, down to earth, mistrustful of speculation. In her native English her speculative Irish mind could wander at will, solve the problems of the world. In English she could do anything. Except, perhaps, what she was supposed to be doing.

She had wanted to be a journalist. She reclined on the puffy pillow. When she worked in Finbar's Hotel that had been her ambition. She had not remembered this in years.

Detta – her name was not Detta then, but Bernadette – had worked as a chambermaid, the summer of 1970. Finbar's had two permanent chambermaids, Mary Mooney and Mary Brazil, but for the summer The Count, as the man who did the hiring and firing had been called, took on an extra. Not that there was that much extra in the way of additional guests. Finbar's Hotel was patronized by commercial travellers, and was always more or less full anyway. If anything there was a slight falling-off during the summer. But Mary Brazil had her fortnight's holidays to take in August. So had Mary Mooney, although nobody, especially not herself, seemed sure whether she would take it or not. Anyway the summer clientele was more demanding than the winter. In the summer the hotel got more couples, people from places like Clonmel or Ballina, on their honeymoon for a week in Dublin. Occasionally a family, Irish emigrants from Manchester or Liverpool or somewhere like that, stayed at the hotel, still bonded enough to want to visit their Irish relations once a year, but rich enough, at last, not to have to actually live in their dour and chilly houses. These people, with their lively, confident English children – dismissed by most Irish people as impossibly bold and cheeky – were much more troublesome than the winter clientele, who did nothing in their rooms except smoke and sleep. (No hanky panky: the rules, pinned to the back of the door, stipulated clearly: 'NO GUESTS IN BEDROOMS UNDER ANY

CIRCUMSTANCES.' The other rules were about drinking in the
bedrooms and vacating the rooms before ten o'clock on the day of
departure. The times of breakfast and dinner, and of daily Mass in St
Paul's and Adam and Eve's, the nearest churches, were also listed.)
These men barely dented their beds. It was a shame, Mary Mooney
remarked, to have to change their sheets after only one night. You
had to, though, even in 1970, even here. But otherwise all you had
to do was empty the ashtray. Commercial travellers had a gift of not
making any dust or any crumples. They were a godsend! Not like
the ones that came in the summer. Oh gonny!

Detta's job was badly paid but very easy. She had to visit twelve
rooms every morning, make the beds and tidy them up. Then in the
evening, at seven, she had to come back to 'turn down the beds' –
what that bellboy had been trying to do this evening. It was a
strange convention, presumably based on the customs of servants in
rich houses: turning back the bed, brushing the mistress's hair, laying
out her clothes for the next day. It always struck her that the logical
next step would be to return when the guest had slipped into the
opened bed, and tuck them in. But this was not required.

Detta had loved her work. She loved visiting the rooms, everyone
of which was different, and seeing what the guests had in them.
There was usually plenty of time to snoop around, to look in the
drawers and wardrobes, examine the contents of suitcases. To her, at
the age of seventeen, personalities seemed infinitely varied and fascinating. Her curiosity about humankind was still insatiable, and her
experience thereof nil. The tiny differences between guests thrilled
her. Although these were nothing more than minor distinctions of
gender, financial and marital status, they seemed to her, empty jug
that she was, profound. She believed she was gaining illuminating
insights into human nature in all its wondrous variety in the bedrooms of Finbar's Hotel. To her these contained God's plenty. Inside
their faded brown walls were locked the psychological secrets of the
universe, and in the pocket of her pink nylon overall was the master
key. One guest travelled with a pair of pyjamas, a razor and rosary
beads. How wonderful that was, how wonderful! Another had two
dressing gowns, three nightgowns, a dozen dresses and pairs of
shoes, four different kinds of perfume, boxes of chocolates, bottles of
lemonade, Mills and Boon books, copies of *Woman's Own*,

Woman's Way and the *Irish Press* and the *Evening Press* every day. The things they carried! Some rooms were filled with the heady aroma of glamorous perfumes, rich soaps – aromas of which Detta was exceedingly fond. Others had one bar of lifebuoy, or even nothing at all, relying on the tiny tablet of dryish, acidic white soap the Finbar's Hotel supplied, one a week per guest and no more – if the guest had a bathroom, that is. (If you didn't get your own bathroom you didn't get your own soap either.) Some guests probably never did wash, while others spent half the day doing it. Some slept till the last minute, dashing down to breakfast at nine thirty, while others were up and off, to Adam and Eve's probably, for seven o'clock Mass or some other form of 1970s masochism (nowadays the notice on the back of the door advised that the gym was open from 6 a.m.). 'I don't know which is the worse,' the cook was prone to say. 'The early birds or the late worms.'

During breaks, of which there were several in the course of the day, Detta retreated to the kitchen, her master key in her pocket, and her bucket, mop and trolley of sheets abandoned on the corridor. There she drank tea with the two Marys and other staff. Mary Mooney, who was aged about forty, and shaped like Mrs Skittle in the Noddy books, round in the body with tiny high-heeled feet and a rubber ball of blonde permed head, regaled them with stories of her health and that of her family, or their ill-health. She had ten children, and lived in one of the new tower blocks in Ballymun. Her husband, Eddie, suffered from nerves, chronic shingles, angina and arthritis. Not surprisingly, he had stayed in bed most of the day for most of his life. Her children had a variety of problems. One of them was in prison, two were expecting, one had spina bifida, one was mentally handicapped. In addition, the lift in the tower block was always broken and Mary had to get herself and these children up and down ten flights of stairs. None of this was funny, Detta knew. But somehow Mary herself made it seem hilarious. 'It's one thing on top of another', she sighed and giggled, as if it was all great gas, designed to provide her with good stories and a bit of a laugh. 'Sure what's the use of complaining?' Detta's own mother said that but she meant the washing machine had packed it in and on top of that the clutch was gone in the Anglia again. Whereas Mary Mooney meant Jim was back in jail for a year on top of Monica having an epileptic fit on Dorset Street and Sharon getting venereal disease. 'Does she make it up?' Detta once asked wide-eyed Mary Brazil, who was twenty-three and whose exclusive topic of conversation was her boyfriend, Michael. 'Oh gonny no!' said Mary. 'I met them, at Mary's mother's funeral. They're just like she says.' 'How does she survive?' 'She does nixers,' Mary Brazil replied. 'She's a handywoman.' Detta did not know what a handywoman was. 'She lays out dead people,' Mary Brazil explained nonchalantly. 'And she delivers babies as well.' Detta was shocked. Mary Brazil stared at her and screwed up her nose. 'You know,' she said, impatiently. 'Some babies. Babies that don't get born in hospital, like.' 'Most of them do, don't they?' Detta was embarrassed. She knew just what Mary Brazil meant but pretended innocence; this was a technique she had used for years to deflect embarrassing disclosures. 'Yeah,' Mary Brazil had had enough of Detta for one day. She shook her head and turned on her hoover.

This was at the first week in July. Detta had been working in the hotel for two weeks. She had saved ten pounds out of the twenty she had earned, towards college in September. Her mother had taken eight, for her keep now that she had got a job, and she had spent two, on bus fares. The sun shone on the quays every morning as she ran along by the river. The air was champagne, the water danced a jig. The old houses, white and yellow and purple and green and pink, smiled like grandparents as she ran along, and the spires of Dublin soared confidently to the enormous sky of her whole waiting life. Her blood raced and her skin glowed and her eyes shone with hope. Every dapple of sunlight, every sweep of spire, promised her that something extraordinary, amazing, stunning, wonderful was just about to happen. The light clean air told her that she was stepping into her future, right now, as you might step from the grey concrete of the quay onto the bridge of a white ocean liner. She was on her way to adult life – a magic island, a treasure trove of riches.

She zapped on the television set. Sports results. The reporters looked very formal, suits and ties, short hairstyles. They spoke excitedly, as if reporting from a war zone. She zapped. An Irish language thing.

Drama or soap, with English subtitles. She let the strange sounds sink into her ears. Everyone spoke at breakneck speed. Only an odd word was comprehensible to her. She had always been bad at Irish. Her mother had hated it, because it was a useless dead language, and because she had been forced to speak it at her old school, Golden Meadow. Her firm belief had been that Irish children should be taught a useful modern language, unburdened by history, instead. Modern meant German. That a knowledge of German was the key to success and happiness was her firmest conviction. When Detta had told this to Piet, her Dutch husband, he had screamed with laughter. Not screamed, he never screamed. He'd had a good laugh, at the idea that German was untrammelled by historical burdens. But he didn't care much about it one way or another. 'A language is just a system of communication,' he said, in his logical way. 'I do not think a language should be regarded as a war criminal, or a hero.'

Detta, who had been a silent, subdued girl, was now a fairly assertive chatterbox in German, Dutch and French, as well as English. She was more European than her mother could ever have dreamed – too European, her mother had suggested, on her infrequent visits to Amsterdam, which she had, after all, hated. Europe was not all it was set up to be, when you actually got there. Mostly just poky apartments, not enough Masses, and overpriced cups of coffee.

Detta zapped. Boom boom, boomboom, boomboom! screamed the signature tune of the newsroom. Here we come with our tales of disaster!

Drama, drama, drama.

She turned it off. What she loved about Holland was what she loved about her husband: its quiet efficiency, its low-key tolerance of human diversity, its reluctance to dramatize everyday situations. 'What happens is silly enough,' Piet said, frequently. 'There is no need to embroider reality.' In Ireland embroidery, often of a very complicated kind, had always been all the rage.

Piet was an electronics engineer, working in a computer firm. Sandy-haired and short, he was as Dutch as a tin of cocoa. He tried to manage life, Detta's and his own, with a light-hearted sense of control, as if it were a rather elementary computer programme, or a football match. The past was over. He did not forget it but grudges were a waste of time. Piet lived in the present, kept his eye on the ball. The only real problem was, he says, over and over again, indecision. 'Decide, decide!' he said impatiently to Detta. 'It doesn't matter what your decision is. Just decide and stick to it.' Kick the ball when it comes your way.

Detta couldn't. For her life was complex, mysterious and unfathomable. Unlike Piet, captain of his fate and of his truth, she believed in the existence of a right answer. It was not on the pitch, but somewhere else, far away – hidden in rolling, electric clouds or buried deep in the radioactive earth of some dark northern forest. Her task was to find it. She believed that if she worried enough she would. Then her questing would be over. She'd be happy.

Piet and Detta had no children. They seldom went to bed together now, but they loved one another as deeply as is possible for a man and a woman. Detta believed this as firmly as she believed anything.

On the tenth of July Conor had come to Finbar's Hotel. Even though he, too, had just completed the Leaving Certificate examination, he'd taken a break with his uncle, playing golf in Kerry, before starting his summer job. He would be the still-room waiter.

As soon as he joined the staff, a rift developed between Detta and the two Marys. They had tolerated her, as one of them, a chambermaid, even though they found her tiresomely secretive, childish and snobby. The fragile solidarity of sisterhood crumpled under the pressure of the much stronger bond of shared Dublin geography: Conor and Detta were from the South Side, the Marys from the other bank of the river. Conor and Detta had done the Leaving, they were summer workers, they spoke in the narrow, cautious accents of their side of the city. The Marys dumped Detta on Conor. What difference did it make, that she was a girl, a chambermaid, like them? She was only pretending anyway. Come October she'd be off to her real life.

Anyway they hadn't quite known what to make of Detta, who was almost pathologically reserved in those days. Conversation had to be dragged from her, word by word. She never volunteered a single bit of information about herself. 'Slippy Tits,' Mary Brazil called her. Mary Mooney, being older, was less judgemental; she had met other Dettas in her day. 'She's quiet,' she said, summing her up in one Hiberno-English word.

Conor was a different kettle of fish. Everyone loved him. He was a good-natured, good-humoured extrovert. He chatted to all and sundry about his family, his past, his plans, and was quick on the draw with witty retorts. But he was a good listener, too, attending to the Marys, The Count and even old Mr FitzSimons with eager ears and eyes full of sympathy and interest. In short, he was just the type of fellow any hotel would be delighted to have on its temporary staff.

In looks he was extremely attractive, but in such an unostentatious, inoffensive way that nobody noticed: they believed they liked him only on account of his personality. He had a big-jawed, blue-eyed, JFK kind of face, and his body was well-knit, coordinated, not gangly or loose like many young men's bodies, and not too tall. Even little men like The Count felt secure beside him. Pleased with life and with himself, he had the gift of disseminating a sense of well-being. He could have been a chat-show host, or the manager of a successful football team, or one of the more popular presidents of the United States. (Or he could have been Detta's father, whom he strongly resembled; she realized this years later.)

'He knows what he wants!' Mary Mooney said, with her chuckle cum sigh. 'Oh go way outa that, he's cute enough!'

This was not quite true. Conor wanted to earn two hundred pounds, towards his college expenses for next year, and he wanted several honours in the Leaving and some sort of special distinction, a scholarship or a prize, as well. But unlike Detta he had not yet decided on a career. Law, medicine, accountancy, were all on his list. So were philosophy, English, and primary teaching. An all-rounder, great at lessons, great at games, he just hadn't been able to make up his mind. 'But I do know I need money,' he said, ruefully. 'Two hundred pounds or bust!'

Acquiring two hundred pounds was not going to be easy, or even possible, as a still-room waiter. The pay was ten pounds a week. No tips came the way of still-room waiters, which is even more of a backstage job than chambermaid – indeed, Detta had not known such a job existed until Conor arrived in the hotel. Soon Conor persuaded The Count to let him work in the bar at weekends, for a few extra pounds and tips. Before long he was working there most nights of the week.

Detta had never had a friend who was a boy before. In fact she had never had a conversation with a boy, at least not a conversation lasting longer than about ten minutes, the time it takes to drink a Fanta lemon in the cloakroom of a school hall. She'd danced with many boys but you couldn't talk much, while dancing. Especially when you didn't know what you were supposed to say to them anyway. Thinking of conversational topics while clenched in a tight embrace and assaulted by very loud music was daunting. Anyway, even when there was no competing band or disc jockey, people usually seemed unable to hear what Detta was saying. A lot of her slow, low comments faded into the air, as ears turned the other way, eager to catch brighter, louder conversation from mouths which were quicker-witted and more in tune with the preoccupations of the moment than Detta ever was.

Conor's ability to listen was his greatest and most astonishing gift as far as she was concerned. He could open her up, turn her on as if she were a radio, and out poured all this guff. In his presence she was transmogrified from being one of the quiet ones to being great gas, from being a bore to being a wit. He asked interesting, intimate questions and actually listened to the answers. Detta had never met anyone like this before in her life.

She sat for hours with him in the kitchen, soothed by the inter-mittent hissing of the silver still, in the quiet evenings between after-dinner tea or coffee and ten o'clock, when Conor knocked off or went to the bar. Talking. They had an ideal subject for openers: the Leaving. A detailed post-mortem of the various examination papers led them through the first stage of their romance. By the time they had analysed Latin, the last exam, Detta was up to her ears in love with Conor. Then they moved on to more thorough discussions of the hotel: the guests, the staff, the food, the architec-ture, the owner, the future, the pay, the exploitation, what they would do if they ran the place. A week of this and Conor was in love with Detta. He asked her to the pictures on his night off, Wednesday. *Butch Cassidy and the Sundance Kid* was the film. They saw it in the Savoy. Conor saw it. Detta couldn't concentrate. The images hopped before her eyes as print does on a page when you are excited. Conor was holding her hand, right through the film. It was the first time she had been touched by any man with whom she was in love. This experience she was unwilling and unable to dilute by concentrating on anything else.

Conor loved the film and wanted to talk about it. She bluffed her way as best she could. Luckily he was enthusiastic enough not to mind. He had a great deal to offer himself, by way of critical analysis. All she had to do was nod from time to time and grunt, 'Ahaw!' She wondered, deliciously, if he would kiss her goodnight.

He didn't. Not that night.

Detta drained her second gin and tonic and decided against taking a third from the minibar. She should stay sober, at least until after the meeting. It was only seven, however, and her appointment was not until nine. She decided to go for a walk and a bite to eat.

She picked a striped blouse, blue and white, and a loose denim skirt from her suitcase. She rubbed her face against the cotton: the fresh shop smell of new clothes always delighted her, and it was a smell you only got before the clothes were worn. Quickly dressed, she slipped her feet into flat open sandals and set off.

Down the pipeline of corridor a youngish, smartly dressed woman was ushering an elderly man into a room. The old man looked terrified, as if he were about to meet some kind of monster. He must have been the girl's father – browbeaten father, apparently. Was this just how frightening it could be to confront your adult child when there was some unassailable gulf between your lives? Was this how it would be for her?

Fear crept in, then gripped her like an ice-cold paw on her chest as she stood on the threshold of the hotel. Her stomach sank, literally: she felt something dropping inside her. And her courage, the ordinary quotidian courage which got her out of bed in the morning, got her into the shower, onto the plane for a holiday, deserted her. It shot out like tea from a flask and this cold, piercing fear rushed in to replace the vacuum. Agrophobia. But it was not agrophobia . It was Dublinaphobia. Hibernophobia.

A terrible story her mother told her about an event at her school, came to her mind, as it often did in moments like these. Her mother had been privileged in her day: her poor parents, small farmers in Clare, had sent her to boarding school, at great cost to themselves. The school was in an old grey manor house, set in woodland in the middle of Ireland. It was there that her mother had spoken Irish. Golden Meadow was the name of that school, a lovely name. But it was not a lovely place, her mother suggested, sighing. It was not lovely, but hard and cold and cruel. She seldom talked about it at all. But occasionally she told a story. The names in the stories changed: Edel Moloney or Annette Finn, Marie Byrne or Rita Darcy. But the story was always the same: a story of beating or starving, the ritualistic humiliation of some child. The children's parents, like Detta's mother's parents, paid fees for this, condoned the abuse. Asked for it. Detta's mother, now dead, had condoned it too, retrospectively. She had condoned it by her silence. Only Detta heard her stories. Her mother told them, not in public, not to protest, not even to her friends or Detta's father. She told the stories when she wanted to hurt her daughter. She must have known that such stories never go away. They wait for their chance in the corners, under the stairs of the mind, jumping in when the good stories flee, at cold moments on thresholds, in the heartbreaking time when the day is ending.

Moments like this. On the steps of the hotel Detta heard the screaming of Golden Meadow. She heard her mother crying. This was the sound of Ireland, Detta thought, drowning out the roar of traffic along the quay. Keening and weeping, children wailing. A longing to flee seized her. In two hours she could be safe in Amsterdam – she could be back in Holland. In Amsterdam she felt safe as she had never felt in Ireland, where the screams of children were mixed with the clay in the parks, were mortared into the faded bricks. Amsterdam had shed its own tears, as she knew well enough. But they were not hers and she couldn't hear them.

A hand alighted on her shoulder.

'Hi!'

It was Karl Brown.

She was pleased to see him.

'Oh hello! How is the fourth floor?'

'I can see the Phoenix Park from my balcony. The biggest park in the universe, it says in my brochure. You might have liked it!'

He had removed his burgundy jacket. Now he was wearing purple. He looked more like a chocolate than ever.

'Well . . .'

'Of course you're afraid of heights!' He laughed.

'Yes.' Detta looked closely at him. 'I sleepwalk sometimes.'

'Ah!' this impressed him. 'Settled in then?'

'I'm perfectly happy.'

'Any plans for dinner tonight?'

'As a matter of fact I have an appointment.'

She felt apologetic, and mildly disappointed. Apologetic that she couldn't have dinner with a complete stranger because she had an appointment with her own flesh and blood! Karl put that hand of his on her arm. Her confusion evaporated. He'd got the gift of touch, this man.

'That's great. Who with?'

She wanted to tell him. But she held back.

'An old schoolfriend.'

He smiled, calmly but too knowingly. He could see through her, he knew everything. Men like that overwhelmed her. Her ego toppled for them because they appealed to it, her libido rose to meet them.

'I'll see you around,' he said, without rancour.

Detta watched him for a minute, as he moved across the bridge a purple blob against the blue sky. Two fat seagulls hovered over his head. It seemed to her that he was flying lightly above the footpath, floating on a swathe of misty air.

Some of her courage had returned. She stepped into the street and strolled across the bridge to the north side of the river. A Mozart air was filling her head, replacing Céline Dion, as she walked. She seemed to hear the music, although she was not musical, could seldom recognize any piece of music, as some people – Piet for instance – could. 'What is it?' he would ask. 'It's Haydn,' she would reply. 'It's Grieg. It's Beethoven's Ninth.' Guessing. Sometimes she hit on the right answer and if she did Piet glowed with a profound, genuine delight which Detta found amusing and puzzling. More of Piet's games: he was such an innocent, by comparison with her. Was that the difference between men and women, or between Dutch and Irish people?

Without him to help her, to quiz her, to inform her, she was unable to name the music in her head, as she sometimes was unable to remember the titles of books she had read in her dreams – aloud even, according to Piet. But a piano pounded in her brain, anger and drama alternating with slow acquiescence. *Allegro, andante, allegro*, went the symphonies. Piet had drummed it into her. *Allegro, andante, allegro*. Like life. Like a story. Like a river.

Detta walked along the footpath on Arran Quay, a walk she had not taken since she was eighteen. Changes? Yes. And no. Apartment blocks, redbrick, with dusty curtains on the windows, had replaced old warehouses and tenements. Otherwise the assortment of pubs – The Croppy Acre, The Legal Eagle – and shops – Heather's Shoes ('Ladies up to Size Eleven'), Bargaintown – seemed familiar, if smarter than she remembered them. The blend of elegance and vulnerability which had always characterized this particular stretch of the river had not changed much, although the details were different.

Few people were about. She met an occasional man or group of men, all of whom eyed her up and down, as if wondering who – or what – she was. Women did not seem to walk along the river, not alone anyway. She pulled her cardigan around her body, the merest frisson of fear galling her stomach. She wished she'd left her bag at home in the hotel.

Arran Quay. St Paul's. How could she have forgotten it? A grey hunk of a city oratory, it had, attached to one of its walls, like a pocked wart, a huge stone cave. In a niche high in this cave stood the calm blue figure of the Virgin, hands outstretched, her smooth face smiling sadly at a smaller, brown, figure kneeling down below: Bernadette – the saint. Not Detta.

Bernadette of Lourdes enjoying a vision of the Virgin. From the angle of a passer-by, Bernadette was a little brown-veiled girl, on her knees, adoring and supplicating the Virgin. Mother of Divine Succour, come to my aid!

She'd need all the supernatural aid she could get, in the Ireland Detta knew.

By a happy, ironic accident of Dublin planning, or lack thereof, the next-door neighbour of the fake grotto of Lourdes was the Four Courts, where the secular powers of Ireland sat and judged, their brand of wisdom heavily inspired by the Roman Catholic Church for most of the twentieth century. A statue of a woman representing Justice stood, austere and stiff, brandishing the weighing scales of objectivity in the yard of the elegant courthouses; the judges might more honestly have placed the Virgin on their threshold, the Virgin with her meek sad smile and her arms haplessly spread, empty of any balance. But at least they had her as a next-door neighbour. (The only Protestant church in the vicinty was the medieval cathedral of Christchurch, thoughtfully concealed from view by the glass and concrete edifice that housed Dublin Corporation. Out of sight, out of mind.)

All that old state-religious stuff has changed, according to report. Ireland was getting more liberal, the fundamental Catholicism which had underpinned its every law for most of the twentieth century diluted by the march of time and by the revelations of flaws in the divine structure itself.

Could you believe it? Detta was sceptical.

Old angers gushed from her. She tried to suppress them. The past is past, Piet, who'd more to be bitter about, said. Again and again and again. Healthy people let go and travel on. They have to. It's not a dress rehearsal, don't wreck it.

The icons were pretty, after all. How sweet and touching the grotto looked, in the midst of all the urbanity, the secularism: it was a a monument to the strength of the spirit, the power of old, simple tradition. Bernadette was lovely, so was the Virgin, in her pale and calming blue, the colour of the nineties. Folk art. That's all it was. If you could forget that it informed the law of the land, that the wan Virgin had ruled and probably still ruled in the Four Courts and the Dáil with a rod of iron, you could enjoy it – just as you would enjoy the women of Iran, quaint and medieval in their long black veils. Forget that they're not allowed to hold jobs, that they're stoned to death if caught in adultery. Take it easy! Enjoy the picturesque look of them.

You're out, you're just a tourist now, Detta said to herself. You escaped from the last bastion of Catholic Europe. You don't need to worry about it anymore. Let the Irish fend for themselves. They always got precisely what they asked for.

What most of them asked for, anyway.

She sighed, and crossed to the riverside, filled with a longing for the solace of water.

When she remembered the Liffey, it was a rippling blue-green river, musically dancing under the blue skies of Dublin. She remembered silver and gold, ripples and dapples of merry light. Riverrun, riverdance, riverfree. Riverlaughing. Annaliviaplurabella and all that.

What she had forgotten was that the Liffey was tidal. Just now the tide was low. Between staunch granite walls the river was the colour of bottle-green, grimy wellington boots. Its surface was covered by a film of oil: reflections of cloud, tree, houses were filtered through greyish-blue whirls and rambling virulent rainbows. A pelmet of dirty ochre kelp dangled from the walls at the hightide mark. Otherwise there was little sign of any natural flora or fauna. No swans or ducks, not even a seagull hovered over the thick opaque water.

It improved as she moved downstream. On Ormond Quay the intimidating wall which barricaded the Liffey for most of its journey through Dublin, hiding it from view unless you were right beside it, was replaced by a white classical balustrade. The gentler architecture encouraged nature: sprays of buddleia sprouted from crevices in the chalky stone of the twisting pilasters here; right in the middle of the river a sooty cormorant swam towards the white curve of bridge, its wings outstretched in the stupid way of cormorants – like the Virgin Mary's arms. It looked lost, far from the sea-rocks which were its natural habitat. But the water must be salty, witness the kelp. And a tang of ozone caught Detta's nostrils, a dark, heartbreaking smell.

Inns Quay. Ormond Quay. The Winding Stair. The Woollen Mills. The Tanning Shop.

Bachelor's Walk was just as she remembered it: pink and yellow, blue and cream, cheerful, redolent of pleasure and glamour. The Knightsbridge Hotel. There were plenty of people here. Young men in blue jeans and shorts – that was new. They usen't to wear shorts in the old days. Girls looked the same as always: long-haired, they teetered along the path in groups or couples, their feet imprisoned in strappy dramatic platform shoes – beautful shoes, gleaming black, brilliant crimson.

Surely I never wore skirts so short?

Surely I did.

But tighter, over a curvier figure, and in the flamboyant colours of the sixties. Shocking pink and brilliant green. Yellow. Gleaming brown with snow white. Girls gleamed and glowed and shone then, with our long plump brown legs, our pointy breasts, our curtains and veils of gleaming hair. All shine and flash and gloss and bounce, a veneer over the terror that lurked inside.

That was before Conor.

Conor hated brash, displaying clothes, loved soft romantic things: misty days in the west of Ireland (preferably on a golf course), traditional music dropping slow into the bleary grey smoke of uncomfortable public houses. Conor liked girlish women – slim and modest, noble and strong, long-haired and beautiful, mysterious but subservient to him – like the girls in his favourite novels by Walter Macken. The feature he loved most about Detta was her Irish colleen hair; well, he wasn't alone in that. Deep red, of a colour often striven for by hairdressers but seldom achieved, it curled and waved in gleaming cascades down to her waist. Conor liked to bury his face in it when he was tired, as he frequently was. Then he would sniff it as if it were opium, and tell Detta she was beautiful.

What he liked best in the way of clothes, Detta soon discovered, were flowery blouses with drawstring waists, flowing green skirts. Shepherdess smocks. And in the way of conversation, he shared with her a predilection for long, serious, anxious discussions about sexual morality followed by long passionate necking and petting (as it was called in the agony columns, although not, of course, by the people doing it, who didn't need to name their activities).

After *Butch Cassidy* the relationship deepened. Detta felt herself descend into love as into a warm, teeming ocean. Further and further down she went, losing sight of everything that floated on top of this sea, losing all sight and all memory of common dry land. She transformed, girl to fish, girl to mermaid. The surface of life, a few weeks ago so all-important, demanding, was gone. She was in another dimension. The dimension of love, a dimension which changed her completely. The reserve which characterized her relationships with almost every other human being vanished. When Conor looked at her, he unlocked a different Detta, a Detta who normally hid inside the skin of the polite, friendly, obliging Detta, the Detta who was diligent and nice, but seldom brilliant, never sparkling. He changed all that. She felt herself glowing and dancing, jokes tripped off her tongue, trite details grew into riveting stories.

He was in love too. Locked into it, as she was, so that every moment of their lives, every possible moment, had to be spent together. But his personality did not change as hers did. She was re-created by him. He remained what he always had been. So it seemed in retrospect. At the time none of this occurred to her at all. All she knew was she was . . . somewhere where she had not been before but where she belonged. Home in love. It was a great gift, she knew it, for the first summer of her grown-up life. The glances of the Marys, of everyone in the hotel, let her know that she was blessed. Shy, amused, awed glances, they were. Not envious in most cases, unless envious of youth. In some situations a young couple in love are irritating, arousing jealousies and other kinds of hostilities. It says much for the atmosphere of Finbar's Hotel and its staff that Detta and Conor endured none of this.

It was partly due to their modesty. At that time, and perhaps at all times, ostentatious displays of sexuality would have irritated people profoundly. Good children of the sixties, Conor and Detta restrained all their natural impulses for physical contact when in public. In private they restrained them too, but not much: broom closets, linen cupboards, empty bedrooms, even the yard – full of beer crates and junk – provided them with spaces in which to give vent to their passion. Their love was so physical it made them cry, as they kissed and hugged and pressed their bodies together. His golden skin, the smell of his arms, the crunch of his hair, filled her with amazement. She ground her teeth together, caught her breath, just thinking of him.

They didn't, of course, have intercourse. That is the word they would have used; the word itself was enough to put anyone off. A cross, hostile word, like barbed wire, a concentration camp. Interrogation. Cross-examination. Coursing. Mothers wagging their tongues, of course of course of course. Of course not.

Contraception. The very word made Detta feel sick: it was so taboo. At that time if a customs officer caught someone trying to sneak a condom, or even a book on what were called 'artificial methods of family planning', into Ireland he could arrest him on the spot. That was the law.

So Conor and Detta kissed and petted, and their bodies fought, valiantly, for what was their natural due. But Conor and Detta had clever, determined minds, trained in denial. No.

Conor's training had been more intense than Detta's; she could see this from the start. He was more conscious of his natural desires but, in inverse relation to that consciousness, more frightened of them. Boys, especially boys like him, were, in those days. Detta did not know what they had been taught, but they had been taught something – unlike the girls, who had been vaguely told not to get pregnant, but given no details at all as to how that disaster might occur. Conor probably knew how. Thus he saw the body as a real enemy, a sort of guerrilla fighter, clever and wily, which would ambush the unwary. He never was unwary. He managed to be in love and on guard at the same time.

Detta knew this, unconsiously, in her mermaid's heart, and her mermaid's heart resented it. But the real Detta, chambermaid and journalist *in spe*, was perfectly content with the way things were. She was getting everything a young girl would want: love, kisses, and what was known as respect – another word the mermaid regarded with sneering distaste.

She crossed the big bridge, O'Connell Bridge. A boy sat by the parapet, a tin box in front of him. He practised a gentle style of begging, passive as a Buddhist monk, his head bowed, his eyes wide and hurt. A note scrawled on a bit of cardboard said 'Homeless. Need money for a hostel.' He was about twelve years of age. At the traffic light crossing at the south side of the bridge a woman wrapped in a cotton shawl pressed a magazine on Detta: 'Buy one, I'm a Romanian refugee,' she supplicated in wheedling voice. She was sallow-skinned, thin and miserable. Wrapped in her shawl was a sleeping baby with a smooth, sleeping face. Catching her breath, Detta gave the woman five pounds for the magazine. She beamed magically, all pearl-white teeth, and said 'Thank you' with feeling. Not 'God bless you,' like the tinker women with the babies used to say long ago.

After a coffee and cherry bun in Bewley's, she walked back on the south side of the river, moving as briskly as she could. Aston

Quay. Wellington Quay. Temple Bar – thousands of summer sandals flowing over cobbled alleys; incense, wine, the smell of cumin. St Winifred's Well. The Poddle.

The cormorant was still in the river at Ormond Quay. But now he was almost submerged in the greasy water. Only his head and big beak protruded. He wriggled his head frantically, and seemed to grin, as he ate a wormy-looking fish – an eel, maybe. Then he dived under. Perhaps he knew what he was doing, after all, marking out this uncontested territory stretch of Liffey as his own?

Wood Quay, Usher's Quay.

Usher's Island – a quay, but on a slight elevation, a hill above the river.

That's where the Ocean Club had been, next door to Number Fifteen, the house of the aunts in Joyce's story, 'The Dead'.

It was not there, of course. Number Fifteen was falling down. In place of the Ocean Club a new apartment block stood. 'Unauthorized cars will be clamped.' Behind the apartments the higgledy-piggledy assortment of smoking buildings that was the Guinness Brewery loomed, comfortingly. The sweet maternal smell of hops drifted from its brick chimneys down to the river.

Cliché of clichés, they did it on the night the results came out, towards the end of August. It was not a big night in Dublin then, as it is now. People were anxious about the results, of course, but nobody queued all night waiting for them. Students called to their school in dribs and drabs, at eleven or twelve o'clock in the day, and the head nun handed them their envelope. Then they smiled and said 'I got six honours' or 'I got it.'

Conor and Detta got seven honours each. Some of them were Cs but nobody had to find out: a respectable veil of discretion covered the finer details. He would get any place he wanted, even the place in medicine which would probably be his final decision. She would get into the journalism course. There was no hassle, and hardly any reason to celebrate, since they had known all along that this would probably be the outcome. Nevertheless they took the night off; The Count insisted, although Conor wanted to work (he'd still got to earn seventy pounds, with five weeks to go).

They went to a film, what they always did on dates, and after-wards, instead of going home, dropped into a nightclub: the Ocean Club, on Usher's Island. They had never gone to such a club before. Once or twice, they'd been to Dr Zhivago's, which was a sort of series of linked white underground caverns, a whirlmaze of psyche-delic lights and loud music. There they had felt silly: it was pointless being in the club, if you were a couple. The disco was for people on the hunt, not for those who had already found their mate. They had been lonely, awkward, disappointed. Conor had sneered at the dresses of the girls, who tried harder than he approved of to be sexy. Detta had laughed, pleased to be demure enough for his good taste, in her flowery smock and long green skirt.

The Ocean Club was not like Dr Zhivago's. They had to knock on the green and blue swirly door to be admitted. Once inside, they found themselves in a dark cave of a room, its walls painted like the outside, swirled and waved, with shells and mermaids and fish, its lights very low. A small jazz band played, deep throbbing tunes that quickly caught Detta under the ribs, jagged her heart. The clientele seemed old; no teenagers, women in skintight dresses, jumpsuits, men in shiny purple shirts, bell-bottoms, white shoes. Some couples danced, slowly, on the little dance floor. Most sat at tables eating or drinking: the places was rich with the smell of fried food.

Conor and Detta sat at a table. A candle flickered in a wine bot-tle, on which an avalanche of red wax drippings had accumulated. She fingered the wax, basked in the flicker of the candle. The smell of fish and chips, overlaid with a faint tinge of wine, thrilled her. The smells were not unfamiliar. The hotel reeked of them. But the ambiance was. This place was different from Finbar's Hotel.

They ate fried scampi and french fries. Conor drank his favourite tipple, milk. Detta considered ordering her usual Fanta lemon, but on a whim said 'Babycham' to the cool, sleepy waitress. Conor started, straightened his back, but relaxed when the music entered his bloodstream.

They danced not just close, which they had done hundreds of times, but dirty – that's what they would have called it. Detta wished she had worn her short skirt and t-shirt, instead of this float-ing gown. She put Conor's hand under the waistband, let him caress her bottom as they swayed around on the floor. She licked his ears.

She pressed so hard into his groin that she came, silently, deliciously, in the middle of the dance floor, her lungs full of the smell of cigarettes and chips, her ears twanging to the jazz.

She'd bridged a gap. Swot to Slag. They were swots, swots from the tips of their toes to the crowns of their heads. In those days, the division existed, unspoken by the girls – usually – but tacitly recognized by most. On that night they transmogrified, as men become swans or monsters or beasts, and became what they normally were not. She did anyway. And he, if not transformed, at least acquiesced. He allowed himself to be carried along on the wave of her wildness. He permitted himself to be seduced.

Afterwards they sneaked into the hotel, into Mr O'Hanlon's room, using Detta's master key, and made love on the bed, on the floor, on the chair. There were no problems at all, for either of them: in all ways, they were ready. The room embraced them. Its chestnut swirly carpet and cigar air encouraged them, its dark uterine redness cradled their first intercourse. (It can be like that, if you are young and healthy, if you are in love. If you have also had the foresight to become a mermaid.) It was the first time, and the best time, for Detta. Perfect sex and perfect love.

Of course she became pregnant. They were seventeen, in peak condition. Of course of course of course of course.

Nine fifteen. Detta was back in her room. She was more critical of her appearance now than she had been a few hours earlier: she had changed from being a compassionate reviewer to a Ku Klux lyncher. In the interim her face seemed to have had it. Face it. Finito. How had she deceived herself? She'd held on fairly well, to her tight skin, her youthful complexion; until a while ago her face had lasted longer than most other parts of her. Even her illness and its terrible treatment had left that bit of her unscathed. But now it too had changed from something smooth and elastic and alive to something like putty-coloured custard. No amount of expensive make-up could ever disguise its jellyish texture, its repulsive puffiness.

Of course it could disguise quite a lot of other flaws, so it was worth putting it on anyway.

She took off her wig and rubbed make-up into her skin; no problem getting up the the hairline when you could take off your hair. Cancer, dare she think it, had some advantages. Carefully she applied eye-shadow, a bit of kohl, lipstick. No mascara: she might be crying later, one way or the other.

She replaced the wig and surveyed herself again. The result was satisfactory: a little slap could work wonders, even on a crock like her, who lacked several crucial bits; she, who had started off believing that life was a tray of jewels waiting to be rifled, had moved through it, losing and gaining, losing and gaining. Losing. *Allegro, andante, allegro.* Most days she felt the balance was even. On bad days she railed against the unfairness of it all. On good days, her heart could still sing.

Paul.

Paul.

Paul.

A solid name. Upstanding, handsome. A curly-haired name, a name of a straight nose and white teeth. A frank open smile of a name. Ships, towers, domes. Soaring cathedrals and dauntless megalithic temples. Rocks steadfast in storm. Horizons. That's what 'Paul' said to her.

Honesty, transparency, decency.

A good name for a judge?

Paul had written to her, asking to meet her, a few months ago. The request frequently came from the child, she was told at the adoption agency. It was up to her to comply or not but . . . they suggested that it would be normal, and kind, to honour it.

Detta had not thought of him for fifteen years, not since she had married Piet. It was not that she had deliberately blocked out the memory. She hadn't needed to: it had simply drifted away from her. Some mothers constructed barriers staunch and elaborate as the Berlin Wall; their psyches worked hard at trying to block painful memories. But Detta hadn't had to work at it. She'd forgotten all about him, her first child, within years of giving birth, without even trying. As if he were a schoolfriend who'd floated out of her life, or any scrap of the past.

The truth was that even now her mind was not on Paul but on Conor. She was about to meet her long-lost son, and all she could dream about was his long-lost father. Paul, poor little baby Paul, had spent years tracing her to her refuge among the tulips. And instead of looking forward to seeing him, wondering what he was like, she was secretly, stupidly, hoping that somehow she would encounter Conor. By some perverted miracle she hoped that when Paul walked into Finbar's Hotel Conor would be at his side, sturdy and tough as he had been in 1970, grinning all over. Her heart, her soul, her body, yearned for him: she had a picture, a feeling, in her, somewhere in her, of a jumper he usually wore, a pale-green lambswool jumper. Her yearning to bury her head on that jumper was intense. A jumper from 1970. That was what she was thinking about on the day of her first meeting in twenty-seven years with her son Paul, who didn't even know that Conor was his father.

And Conor did not know either. She had never told him about the baby. After the night in the river club he had grown distant, not because of the sex in Mr O Hanlon's room, but because of her transformation. Detta the slut. Conor did not want a slut in his arms, in his life. All his conditioning warned him against that. What he wanted was his career, and a wife who would be vivacious and modest, chaste and girlish, good-humoured and demure. A Walter Macken girl. Controllable. Predictable. All those able things. Not a wildcard. Not Detta, of the two characters.

When she found out she was pregnant, she had, however, asked him to marry her. His answer was that he loved her deeply; she was a marvellous girl. These were his very words, spoken in his mellifluous, seductive voice. 'Marvellous girl.' When Detta heard them she felt sick. She knew there was no hope. She was a marvellous girl and he would always be grateful, eternally grateful, for knowing her. Tears were in his voice as he spoke. Something in Detta turned to ice. By the time he was telling her that he planned to become a priest, all she wanted to do was run away from him, run faster than she had ever run before. She wanted to swim in a tempestuous ocean, or jump from a cliff into a deep cold snowdrift. She wanted to be as far away from him as she ever could be.

Later she considered her options. It was clear to her that she could force him to marry her merely by telling him about the baby.

He would not have a moment's hesitation; if she told him, the marriage would occur at the first opportunity. The choice was all hers. She could probably have forced him anyway, by insisting on the rights of her love. He would have given in: that business about wanting to be a priest was probably a whim. In a month he'd change his mind.

But she didn't go back to him. There was something in the arch of his back, the distancing of his glance, the cold terror of the phrase 'marvellous girl', that prevented her. It had all been easy for them: they had found each other and existed in a shell of understanding. Once they had had sex, the understanding had vanished. She had already seen it, before she knew about the pregnancy. She knew he did not like her anymore, although sometimes he fell, fell into her, longed for her, longed for sex with her. But it was against his better nature.

His better nature was what she no longer wanted, not on its own, with its critical apparatus polished and honed, ready to hate her if she fell into lasciviousness – if she reverted to the Ocean Club.

Sulking, she turned her back on him.

She told her mother about the pregnancy. 'This is the worst thing that could ever have happened to me,' her mother said. She had cried angry tears of shame. 'What will I say to people?'

Later her mother regretted her reaction. She tried to help Detta. Detta punished her, accepting the minimum of assistance. She, too, was ashamed. Also arrogant, proud, and independent. Damage had been done. She was in no hurry to forgive.

That her education would be postponed or ended was accepted unquestioningly by herself and her parents. She took a a job in a solicitor's office, as a receptionist, and rented a tiny bedsitter in Ranelagh, much to her parents' upset. When she was seven months pregnant, and the bump began to show, her boss called her into his office. He asked her if she expected to marry shortly, and explained that he had a policy, in common with the Civil Service and most organizations, of not employing married women. Detta said she was not engaged or intending to marry. 'I am asking you to resign anyway,' was what he said. 'I will give you a good reference.'

Ever after Detta wished, more heartily than she wished most

things, that she had replied 'Don't bother.' But she had accepted the reference silently, and left.

There was a Mother and Baby Home, a Magdalen Home, in Donnybrook, not far from where she lived. Instead of going home to her mother, she went there. The idea of approaching Mary Mooney never crossed her mind.

At the home, a friendly Reverend Mother talked to her. This nun advised Detta not to take a place in the home, not giving any special reason: Detta, thinking of the institution as a kind of hospital, got the impression that there were no vacancies, just then. If she called some other time, perhaps . . . Instead of taking her in, the nun gave Detta away, to a family, a kind of charitable foster family of a type which flourished in Ireland at that time, specializing in this exotic form of charity: putting up unmarried mothers while they waited to have their babies in secret. The family, Yvonne and Mick Clancy, lived in a yellow bungalow outside Athlone: their garden, where Detta hung out washing, since housework by the unmarried mother was part of the deal, sloped down to the Shannon. It was May then, the garden was ablaze with forsythia and laburnum, intoxicating lilacs. Detta had sat there, in the sun, drinking tea and chatting with Yvonne. Later, when Detta had heard about the Magdalen Homes, the cruelty of them, the ill-treatment meted out to the girls, she had felt an overwhelming guilt. She could have been washing dirty clothes and scrubbing floors (a bit like Finbar's Hotel, only with shame and pain instead of fun and the Marys, money and Conor). Instead she sat among the lilacs, listening to the blackbirds, watching the sun dance on the shirred blue water of the Shannon. She never found out why this was her fate, while other girls got the dirty linen and harsh words. Luck, perhaps – or perhaps her seven honours, which she had mentioned to the nun, and her new cream bouclé coat and her Clonskeagh accent?

She could now remember the Clancy's riverside garden better than her own baby, whom she had, after a painful labour – muscles too strong and none of the hope for the birth which can transform normal labour to an adventurous challenge: The birth itself had been a release rather than the moment of great joy mothers speak of. It is true that Detta had felt a great rush of love when she looked at the baby, a sort of love she had never known before (or since). She had started to cry at that moment. She had never wept so profusely. A splashing, exuberant fountain of maternal love gushed out of her. 'You're exhausted,' the midwife had said, brusquely, fearing the joy in Detta's tears. 'You'll feel better when you get some sleep. We'll look after this big bruiser!' Bruiser. Detta winced. She wept on, but her tears became thin and bitter, and gave her no relief.

A week after the birth she handed him over: Conn, she had called him, after his father. The adopting parents were allowed to replace her name for him with one of their own choosing. They did.

Detta was eighteen. The two big loves of her life were over. That is what she thought. She went to England, to London, where she got a job with one of the new computer companies: the excellent reference from her former boss helped. There, more than ten years later, she met Piet, who was over demonstrating new programmes. He was older than her, and divorced from his first wife. She fell in love with him and after a while returned with him to Holland. That is her official biography, neat as a complex sentence.

At twenty to nine she bounced downstairs. Karl Brown was in the foyer as she passed, looking at a woman who sat in an armchair, opposite the entrance, writing busily on a laptop computer. Detta nodded to Karl. She would have a drink with him tomorrow. She promised herself this in order to put what was about to happen into perspective. Whatever the outcome, this was just one night in her life. Tomorrow would come along. Tomorrow would include a drink with Karl, if nothing more, as well as whatever else fate had in store for her.

She supposed the Irish Bar was the right place to wait, and went in there. It was less Irish than the name suggested, warm and comfortable; through stained glass windows coloured lozenges of light fell, dappling its deep soft seats. The unsinkable *Titanic* song was playing, inevitably. But its sentimental melody was all but drowned by a tumult of human noise, coming from a crowd gathered in the corner – one of those Dublin stag nights that even the Dutch had heard about? She looked more carefully. All the members of the

party looked elderly. It must be some sort of old folks' celebration –
a retirement, perhaps.

An arrow pointed to 'Fiona's Bar' at the far side of the dining
room. Detta went and had a look at it: it was small and cosy, with
tiny glass tables and bentwood chairs; the bar was dominated by a
huge array of gleaming bottles. The place seemed to be modelled on
an Italian or French café, which Detta always found mildly intimidating, probably because dozens of curious male eyes looked up
from their drinks or their dominoes or their cards and stared at her
whenever she walked into one. Only a few people sat in Fiona's bar
and none of them paid any attention at all to Detta. But she decided
to return to the Irish Bar, where the plush seats were comforting.

She sat as far away from the crowd in the corner as she could.
They were a noisy lot, however, and impossible to ignore for long.
Her eyes wandered from them to the doorway, from the doorway to
them. Two or three of them looked familiar, but she could not place
them. Then a woman shaped like a round skittle, with a small head
of yellow pin curls, walked across the room to the corner and said
'Howareyez! Sorry I'm late but . . .' Detta blenched. It was Mary
Mooney.

She looked at the crowd in the corner more carefully. Other
faces began to swim into focus, find their eternal structures, their
names. There was Mary Brazil. And The Count, who must be about
ninety.

She had thought everything and everyone had disappeared, had
sunk into the rubble of the old Finbar's Hotel. But the opposite was
the case.

Maybe she should go somewhere else? She didn't want to meet
her long-lost son in full view of Mary Brazil and Mary Mooney.
What had possessed her to select Finbar's Hotel at all? How could
she have believed that all the old staff would have gone, just because
time had passed and the hotel had been rebuilt and was owned by
Dutch rock stars or whatever they were? Well. Because she couldn't
imagine a Dutch rock star, or any other Dutch person, employing
the likes of Mary Mooney or Mary Brazil, perhaps, or any of the
old crowd? That some sort of reunion was going on the very night
she had picked to visit was a horrible coincidence, that was all.
Don't exaggerate!

She couldn't move from her spot. This was the spot Paul had meant. If he really came, if the meeting happened, it would have to happen right here, with Mary Mooney and Mary Brazil and The Count and goodness knows who else viewing it from standside seats.

Her eyes swung around to the door again. No sign.

Nine thirty. Conor was always late for things, she recalled. That was his style. The Irish way, different from the Dutch. Piet called when he said he would: nine meant nine. If Paul was late it was because he was Irish, not because he was unreliable. You had to accept these cultural differences.

Nevertheless she was anxious, so anxious that she had a cramp of nervousness in her stomach.

She went to the bar and ordered a glass of port. While she was there, Mary Brazil came up and said: 'Excuse me! Don't I know you from somewhere?'

Detta looked at her. She had seemed so much older than herself in the past, but in fact she was almost the same age. Her black hair was still black, her sallow skin unwrinkled. Had she married that boyfriend, Michael? Detta would have liked to find out but she said 'No. I don't believe you do.' Her blonde cap of hair protected her privacy. Mary Brazil smiled uneasily, gave Detta a scrutinizing look, and returned to her corner.

Nine forty-five.

It struck Detta that he might not come. Cold feet at the last minute. It wouldn't be easy for him either, meeting his long-lost mother. What resentments he might harbour against her! When she 'gave him up', as they expressed it then, it seemed for the best. It wasn't as if she were giving him up to an orphanage, although the place where she had the baby reminded her of the orphanages, of the terrible school her mother had told her about, the dark hatred of children which had characterized Ireland's past. She knew he was being placed with a good family. She knew their names, their occupations: the man was a librarian, the woman a teacher. You could ask for nothing more respectable, more humane, it had seemed to her. They had a house in Bray, close to the seafront. She felt the sacrifice was all hers, something she was doing purely for the sake of the baby.

114

But the baby might see things differently. Maybe he hadn't liked his adoptive parents? If such things did not work out, it would be easy to point the finger of blame at the mother. Who else could you blame, especially in this case, where the father did not even know about his son?

A pang of guilt caught her there, as well. Fathers. They had changed completely now, them as well as everything else. In 1970, it would not have occurred to her that Conor might have wanted to know he had a child. She had assumed that a child would spell disaster for him, for any young man. All she had heard was of how young men bolted, deserted, cried that the child wasn't really theirs. The idea that young men would demand paternity rights, would want to have the child, would have seemed laughable. Why would they? Young men didn't even want to get married, was the attitude her mother had inculcated in her. As a girl she would have to snare them into it in some way. Mothers fretted that all this free love would let them off the hook entirely. Detta's own mother predicted that men would never get married at all, if they didn't have to. Why would they, if they could have sex for free? Without paying for all that with wedding rings and jobs for life and mortgages and babies? The society was misogynistic then; that was recognized by the budding, despised, women's libbers, who already then were creating a flutter of protest against the deeply ingrained hatred and disparagement of girls and women in Irish society. But the same society hated men as well, in a subversive, mysterious way. The women, resentful of all other women, often mistrusted and derided men. They were regarded as belonging to another species altogether, lacking all human feeling, childish, boorish creatures to be tricked and manipulated, then reeled-in and ruled for life. That was what Detta's mother had taught her. Detta's mother did not believe that true love was possible, and forced Detta to share that belief, in spite of all evidence to the contrary.

Being a martyr to men was what Detta had been taught she would be, and she fulfilled her mother's expectations. Being an abandoned unmarried mother was the ultimate fulfilment of her mother's expectations – so ready was Detta for the role that that she failed to notice that it was she who had done all the abandoning. What a martyr she had felt, living in her pathetic bedsitter, going off to the place in Athlone when she was in the eighth month. What a heroic, saintly, put-upon Irishwoman! Everyone she met encouraged this point of view. Yvonne, in Athlone, had gloated in Christian sympathy. It dripped from her like the honey-flowers from her laburnums. 'You poor love,' she had gushed. 'It is all very hard for you, pet, but it will soon be over, and all for the best.' She fell short of calling it a 'learning experience' but only because the phrase was then unknown, at least in Athlone.

Detta could have just married Conor. He had not, as she'd anticipated, become a priest. She'd found out that he left the seminary after two years, and studied medicine. He could have managed that, married to her, with a baby. Conor was the kind who would have coped, and so was she. She had done well in spite of every obstacle. People survive, and prosper. Most people – the Romanian woman flashed through her mind, a reminder that there were exceptions to this rule.

She should trace Conor. Merely to satisfy her curiosity.

It wouldn't be hard. He was probably listed in the telephone directory. She could ring him after meeting Paul. She promised herself she would. After meeting Paul. Another task for tomorrow.

Nine fifty-five. Detta got up, her stomach still aching, and went to the door of the bar. The woman with the laptop was still sitting in the foyer, although she had stopped typing. She was looking furtively around the foyer, obviously searching for someone herself. For a dark and terrifying minute, Detta wondered if she could possibly be some emissary from Paul, sent to give his excuses? His adoptive mother, perhaps? Clenching her stomach, she walked in front of the woman, giving her a good view. But the woman got up and walked away, completely ignoring her.

'What happens is silly enough,' said Piet's voice, lightly mocking, in Detta's head. 'Don't paint the devil on the wall.'

Piet had encouraged her to come to Dublin and meet Paul, but urged her not to take the whole thing too seriously. 'Of course I won't!' Detta had retorted. 'You know me, carefree as a butterfly!'

Piet was Jewish as well as Dutch, or had been. His mother had given him to a childless gentile couple when he was born, in 1944.

Later that year she died, in a concentration camp. Abandonment by his mother had been Piet's salvation.

None of this seemed to have marked him. He was without bitterness. That is why Detta loved him, or one of the reasons.

She returned to her seat in the bar, deciding to give Paul another fifteen minutes. Then she would decide what to do: ring Piet and ask him for advice, comfort herself with his sound common sense. Or ring Karl and suggest that they have dinner, after all, and take the risk that involved. Or go back to her lonely barque of a bed, and cry herself to sleep.

Then Conor walked into the bar.

Conor, exactly as he was thirty years ago. Taller, perhaps, but with his sandy skin, his thick reddish hair, his JFK eyes and jaw. He was wearing jeans and a blue shirt, a waistcoat. He glanced around the room.

Detta's eyes widened, when she saw him. He opened his arms. She stood up and he moved quickly, running, towards her.

'It's Paul?' she asked, stupidly.

'Don't you know me, mother?' he laughed and took her in his arms. Detta put her head on his shoulders.

In her head the crying of the children quietened.

Paul was smiling. He was handsome, easy, smooth skinned, smiling. Competent: Conor's son. He knew how to handle a situation, even one as awkward as this.

'You look beautiful,' he held her away from him, at arm's length. 'You're just like I imagined you!'

This is too easy, Detta began to think. There should be hesitation, misunderststanding. He should be disreputable, impoverished, mean. And disappointed.

She saw Karl Brown at the bar, looking quizzically at her. He raised his glass, a shining flute of champagne.

She heard Piet's voice in her memory saying 'Everything turns out for the best!'

Keeping her hands on Paul's elbows, she moved back to gaze at him.

Karl was observing her and Paul with shameless curiosity, as, indeed, were most people in the room. Detta's eye wandered, uneasily, to the old folk in the corner. Mary Mooney was staring over, smiling sentimentally, taking it all in: she probably guessed everthing. Detta grinned and Mary winked. Mary Mooney! She'd go over and talk to her later, insofar as later existed anymore.

Later and then became now.

Detta holds her baby up. She counts his eyes and his ears and his fingers and his toes. She turns him round and looks at the strip of fair hair on his back. She puts him to her breast and lets him suck.

'Oh, I love you!' she says. She says. She says.

This is it.

This is the moment, the moment the mothers talked about: the lightning flash of heaven, the blissful glimpse of eternity. Twenty-seven years late, but she is getting it again: the happiest minute of human life. Couldn't she could find a more original way to express herself, to give voice to the amazing burst of emotion that washes through her, stronger than anything she has ever felt? But she can't find better words. She can speak English, Dutch, French and German. A smattering of Italian. But none of these languages help her. She would like to compose a symphony, or even a song. She would like to burst into a passionate poem.

The Céline Dion song has been switched off. Someone is singing an Irish song at last, some old air jazzed up to suit the new mood of Ireland, the Ireland where it's OK to be Irish, where it's the cool thing to be. Mary Mooney is joining in in the song: she always had an astonishingly sweet voice, Detta remembers. It used to soar down the corridors as she moved around, mop and bucket clinking. 'I dreamt I dwelt in marble halls,' she would sing, in her high soprano. 'My young love said to me my mother won't mind,' used to float out from the downstairs toilet. 'Oh Danny Boy!' accompanied the hoover, the notes dipping and swooning as the machine roared.

Karl Brown is smiling from the bar, sipping his champagne, his purple jacket glowing. A golden light shines from him and beams across at Detta and Paul, at Paul and Detta, at Detta and Paul, at Paul, Detta's son, and Detta, Paul's mother. Mary Mooney sings with joy and surprise isn't life a gas who would have thought and is that what's his name the one who was going to be the priest he hasn't changed a bit and neither have you Detta who used to have long red hair and two breasts and a boyfriend and a baby, Detta who once was young with all her life before her, Detta who once was a chambermaid called Bernadette.

Detta closes her eyes.

From the tight shells of her closed eyes warm tears fall and from her mouth fall the tawdry, overused tepid words, the only words she has.

'I love you too,' Detta's son, Paul who once was Conn, says. His body is warm, his voice is warm, his hug is warm around her.

Peonies burgeoning pink and powerful narcissi cream as newbirth tulips roses myrtle madness sunlight starlight moonlight riverlight new grass new hay cornfields cornoceans sapphires rubies emeralds diamonds *eine kleine Nachtmusik* oh Danny Boy she loves you

I love you too! I love you too!

Detta's soul explodes. In a million singing fragments it rockets to the farthest stars.

10

THE GARDEN OF EDEN

In the end, David simply said, 'I am going.' And Carmelita knew what he meant.

'All right,' she replied. She had been waiting for this announcement for twelve years. She had feared it, postponed it, protested against it, and also, at other times, of course wanted it, craved it, paved the way for it. Now, this now, this minute, sitting, appropriately, at the kitchen table (*ad mensa*. What's the Latin for 'at', she wondered idly), it was nothing but a bald fact, like the sun that shone on the lawn outside like the marigold in the window-box, like the wine-glass of water on the blue checked cloth.

David stood up, leaving a little food on his plate, and went upstairs. Carmelita sat, gazing absently out the window. The laburnum was dropping black pods on the yard. The lobelia had withered. A few montbretiae bloomed with their characteristic brilliance in the euphemistically named rockery but mostly the garden was on the wane. Middle August, and hardly a thing left in it. After nine years in the house. And garden. David usually took care of the garden. The split would be mainly *ad hortis*, actually, she thought calmly, pleased to remember this word, if not its cases. He'd never done anything much at the table except eaten the food she'd cooked.

Carmelita considered the garden next door as she often did. It was the horticultural tour de force of the neighbourhood: tender velvet lawn, bright but not gaudy borders, shrubs in all the right corners, flowering or leafing in a happy sequence of colours, scents and textures. Patio, arbour, roses clambering over trellis, geraniums in great carved terracotta pots. An ornate Victorian conservatory.

Carmelita envied them, those next door. She coveted that garden. She craved it passionately.

David popped his head in and said: 'I'm off now. Goodbye!' His heavy step sounded on the hail floor. The door opened and then shut slowly and sadly, but firmly.

Carmelita stopped thinking about the garden next door. She got up and plugged in the kettle and made a cup of tea. When it was ready, she carried it out to the garden, her own garden, and sat down at the table there. A white plastic table with a green sun umbrella, and a few odd, mismatched lawnchairs surrounding it. She sat and looked at her shrubs, her flowers, her trees, and the sky. The evening sky in early autumn, the middle ages of the year. The little bit she could see in the gap between the sycamores was a pale wishy-washy pink. The sun had already disappeared behind the roofs of the houses on the next road. The summer is over, well and truly over, she thought and a dreadful last-rose-of-summer sentiment of loss and bereavement overwhelmed her for a few minutes. But she did not wallow in it; she waited for it to pass, because she was so accustomed to this sensation.

Periodically, every year from about the tenth of August to the beginning of September it struck. Her last-rose-of-summer depression. She was very sensitive to seasonal cycles, like a lot of women who live in suburbs. The beginning of nice ones, like spring or summer, brought jubilance. The end of nice ones – and there is only one season that really ends – was like a great tragedy which experience seemed to exaggerate rather than assuage. And August seemed much more of an ending, so much gloomier, than September, which had its own character and self-confidence and was the beginning of something again, even if it was something not very good. School. Frost. Long dark nights.

Carmelita and David had been married for twelve years. Oh yes! How time flew. It seemed no length at all since their wedding. Since that time of being in love with David. Perhaps time does not exist when the emotions are concerned. On the other hand it was aeons ago; its trappings belonged to history. That ceremony in the registry office in Kildare Street. The drinks afterwards in the Shelbourne, with everyone dressed up somehow. The bridesmaid in white pants and a navy striped t-shirt had looked odd, certainly. Carmelita could have killed her. But most of them had made a respectable effort with flowery dresses and hats. Outmoded. Dated. Ancient.

David had been as always: smiling broadly, jocular and in full control. He was smart and quick witted, David. She had basked in that, in his protection. He was never at a loss. His decisions were, almost invariably, the correct ones. And he never regretted them, as a matter of principle.

The decision to get married had not been his, of course, but hers. And her decisions were frequently wrong, she had found out as her life progressed. Usually they were irrational, whereas David's would as a rule be the opposite. It had seemed terribly necessary to marry him at that time twelve years ago, though. She had been pregnant, but that was not why. It had seemed necessary before the pregnancy, which was an effect, not a cause, of the need. Marriage to David had seemed to be her only salvation, the only course open to her in life. Life without him, she thought, was unthinkable. She would die without him. She would wither up and cease to exist.

And indeed her expecations had been fulfilled. Marriage had brought happiness and activity. Life had been full as a tick. It ticked, ticked all day, all night. There was never a moment's idleness. She had been so busy, so very busy, for several years. So busy that she had not time to consider whether she was happy or not.

Only in retrospect did she realize how happy she had been during that hectic time. Not having time to think of it, that had been her happiness, it seemed. Not having time to bless herself.

She was not busy anymore.

The garden was empty before her eyes. Friday evening. She had the weekend free, three nights, two whole days, all for herself.

She walked over to the fence dividing her garden from the garden of Eden. She did this every night, because the neighbours were away on their fortnight's holiday in Greece. There was a broken place on the fence – God knows how they had let it remain broken – over which she could peer and get a perfect view.

The first sight of it broke upon her like a peaceful oriental vision: there was a quietness in this garden, partly because it was quiet since there was nobody in it, but more because of its perfection. The greenest grass. The fluid forms of the bushes. The pale pinks, yellows, lilacs of the flowers. It was in no way a busy garden, although it required much business to achieve the effect it created. Like a beautiful, rich room, upon which endless attention and expense has been lavished, it looked natural and spontaneous.

David had driven off in the car. She had heard him starting it, she remembered, just after the door shut. He was possibly far away by now. The thought that there was no longer a car crossed her mind, like a slight shadow, and disappeared. Who needs a car?

She began to climb the fence. A thin wooden fence. It was not difficult, because it had wires attached to it, bits of broken chicken wire up which she had once tried to grow woodbine but without success.

She swung herself over the narrow top and jumped on to the pale red pavingstones of the patio next door. At first she stood and looked around at everything she had seen so often from the other side of the fence. The palm and elephant grass just where the patio met the lawn. The green hose lying on the slabs. The pots of deeply pink geraniums all around. And, placed at interesting vantage points further down the garden, beds of lupins, hollyhocks, columbines and canterbury bells, their colours deep and velvet, their heads bowing, one to the other, like coquettish ladies at some brilliantly flirtatious court. She breathed deeply, and perfume from mignonette, honey-suckle and escallonia filled her lungs, along with a headier, more intoxicating air: somehing like incense.

She walked slowly along the lawn. The greenness of it soaked into her skin; she could feel her body absorbing it. It was like swim-ming softly, breaststroking through a long aquamarine pool. Or through a cloud. Although naturally she had never swum in a cloud.

She sat on the grass for a minute. It was dampish. She could feel the wet seeping into her skirt. A ladybird came and crawled along her leg, one of the more unusual yellow ladybirds which, in their gay spotted shells, reminded Carmelita of fashionably rigged-out toddlers. It was a great year for these insects. All the gardens were infested with them. They were tolerated even by the best gardeners on account of their appetite for greenflies. All years were great years for greenfly.

Carmelita stayed on the grass for a long time. Then she got up and left using the same route and technique she'd employed in entry. Before she left she cut three slips from the geraniums, whose pink blossoms rested like hot fluttering butterifies on their turgid foliage. And when she got to her own side of the fence, she potted the slips in terracotta plastic pots, in peat moss, and put them on the window sill to root. She had heard from a woman she'd met once on a plane to London that stolen slips did best.

She went to bed. The house creaked a lot. Some doors banged because a window was open. She thought about burglars. She believed in burglars, but her image of them, like her childhood images of God and the Devil, was vague. They were male, they would break glass, they would burst into her bedroom and . . .'

Lulled by such creaks and bangs and ideas, she fell asleep.

The next day would have been long and empty, had she not decided in the morning that she really must go shopping. So she took the bus into the city centre and spent the whole day walking around the shops, trying on clothes, examining furniture and rugs. Time passes very quickly in town, and she remembered the Saturdays of her youth, her later youth that it is, when she had lived with her mother and had her job, the job she still had. Shop after shop, garment after garment. Bought, worn a few times, discarded.

She bought a white linen suit. And a bag of peaches. And a packet of incense sticks.

And several small terracotta pots.

That evening, she watched television and cut three slips of escallonia in the garden next door.

She burned the incense, thinking how David hated incense or anything that seemed cheap and eastern, like curried eggs and the novels of Hesse and Indian rugs. She drank some red wine but it was sour as it usually is if you buy a cheap bottle in a supermarket and she could not take more than one glass.

Her thoughts were less of burglars as she lay in bed, and more of the past. Not the past with David, which hardly seemed like past. But of her childhood, of her teenage years which seemed, in retrospect, serene and carefree. She also thought about her slips and planned the future of her garden. Every mickle makes a muckle, she thought, and eventually it will look like theirs next door. Patience is a virtue.

Carmelita was not an especially patient woman, and on Sunday she went to a garden centre and bought a palm tree and a blue hydrangea (she'd never fancied the pink) and came home and planted them on the back lawn. And that night, after dark, she stole a large carved terracotta pot from the garden next door. But for the time being she put it in her bedroom where the next-door neighbours were not likely to see it.

That night as she lay in bed she thought of the next-door neighbours. They would not have seen the pot if she'd put it in the hall or the living room either, she thought, because they did not visit her house. The reason was, she and David had had such fearful rows in the year or two after the accident. Carmelita had been given to screaming loudly in the middle of the night. She used to accuse David of all kinds of awful things: not being sensitive, not caring about her, not giving her the love she needed. She had ranted and raved and screamed at the top of her voice, and sometimes David had hit her. To shut her up. Battered. She had been a battered wife, according to a certain point of view. In her own estimation, in retrospect but even at the time, she could justify David's hitting her. They always say they've been provoked. But in his case it was, she suspected, true. Anyway invariably she had hit him back, and not infrequently she had hit him first. They had been like two boys scuffling in the school playground.

Except that the sound effects were higher pitched and more alarming.

They heard. She knew they must have heard. It was so embarrassing. She hadn't wanted to speak to them. She didn't speak to them, or have cups of tea with them, or invite them in for a drink on Christmas Eve.

It had all stopped long ago. There was no noise, no screaming. No fighting at all. But the pattern was set. No neighbourliness. No visits.

Lulled by these thoughts she fell asleep.

The next morning was Monday and Carmelita was supposed to get up and go to work. She worked in a bank. She was a cashier. It was not as boring to her now as it had been when she'd started it: she enjoyed saying hello to the customers, she liked to be nice and friendly and make them feel at ease, which is not how most people feel in a bank. And also, over the years, she had grown fond of her colleagues and of her salary.

But this morning she did not go to work. She got up at the usual time of eight o'clock and went down and had her coffee. But when the time for leaving the house came, she did not go. Instead she went into the garden. She examined the slips: none of them had withered so far, which she took to be a good sign. Now she had fuchsia, escallonia, and geraniums on the go. She climbed over the fence and looked around. The garden next door looked even more wonderful than usual in the early morning light. The fresh clean sunshine, the unsullied air of start of day, suited its own spick and span, cared for, character. It was in its element.

Carmelita walked all around it, simply admiring. She no longer felt any envy or covetousness, she realized, and supposed it must be because she knew that soon – or at least eventually – she was going to have her own beautiful garden. As beautiful as this. Or more beautiful? No. Just the same.

What would she take? She remembered that they were due home the day after tomorrow, so her time in the garden was limited, and she would have to choose exactly what she wanted now. She looked at dahlias, and lupins, and tearoses. Broom and rose of Sharon and a shrub she did not know the name of which had greenish reddish leaves and huge fluffy red balls. She looked at elephant grass and marram grass and cordeliine.

In the end, she cried 'Ah!' Because she saw it. Just exactly what she had wanted all the time. How odd that she had not seen it before; how very odd. In the corner of the patio, propped up against the wall, a small tricycle belonging to the youngest child next door. There were three children, two girls and a boy. The boy was the youngest. He was four, and this was his bicycle.

She grabbed it and let it down over the fence as gently as she could. Then she herself climbed over, and carried the tricycle up to her bedroom, where she put it on the floor just beside the bed.

After the accident, all Raymond's things had been given away. Absolutely everything; David had thought it was better that way. It was all as bad as it could be. They didn't need reminders, he had said, packing the toys and the clothes and things, Raymond's things, into boxes for the travellers who called to the door every Saturday, regular as clockwork.

There were the photographs, of course, but only in albums. None out on the sideboard, none displayed with the other photographs on the mantelpiece. They had to get over it. They had to forget.

She lay in bed for a while, thinking about her slips and glancing at the tricycle from time to time. Then she searched in the drawers of David's desk for the albums. She selected three of the nicest pictures, showing Raymond at one, three and seven and a half, just after he'd made his First Communion and just before he'd died. She propped them up on her dressing table where she could see them at night before going to sleep and in the morning as soon as she awoke. She'd get some frames for them later. Later today, or maybe tomorrow, or maybe she'd ask David to get them.

Because of course he was going to come back. And David came back that very night, because he'd rung the office and – she hadn't been there, and because he couldn't cook, and for various other reasons. His decisions were usually rational, and usually correct, and he hardly ever regretted them, on principle.

11

FULFILMENT

Killiney is the anglicization of *Cill Inion Léinín*, the chapel of the daughter of Léinín. Who she was I do not know. Perhaps a saint like Gobnait of Cill Ghobnait. Or a princess like Isolde of Chapelizod. Perhaps she was just the daughter of a butcher, born in the Coombe, moving out to Killiney to demonstrate her upward social mobility, like many of those who live there. It is a fashionable address. An inconvenient, overcrowded, unplanned jumble of estates, possessing, nevertheless, a certain social cachet. It was that which drew me to it, first.

Some people think I came for the scenery. My house is practically on the beach. From the front room I can gaze at Bray Head, spectacular for a suburban view. The strand itself unwinds in a silver ribbon from the bathroom window. It is long and composed of coarse grains of sand which cut your feet if you walk barefoot thereon. I never do. There is no reason to do so unless you want to swim. And swimming from Killiney Strand is an activity which loses much of its appeal as soon as the hulking grey monster lurking halfway along the stretch of golden shingle is recognized for what it is: an ineffectual sewage treatment plant. Shit from Shankill, nuclear waste from Windscale, can have a dissuasive effect. On me, at least. Many people revel in it, however, and emerge from the sea, not deformed, but rarely quite the same as they were before they ventured in. Necks swell, pimples speckle peaches-and-cream, nipples invert and toes turn inward. And worse.

Killiney means much to me. I have lived there for thirteen years and would never forsake it. Not because I cherish any affection for the locality. The roads meandering drunkenly up and down the hill, the opulent villas perched like puffins on the edge of the cliff, the mean houses marshalled in regiments across the flatlands; these, in their essential lack of harmony, disturb my sense of the symmetrical, which is acute. Neither do I cling to Killiney because it provides me with congenial companions. I live in near isolation, enjoying little or no contact with my neighbours, apart from the occasional unavoidable shoulder rub with the post- or milkman. Some stalwart of the local residents' association drops the community newsletter, *KRAM*, through my letterbox every month. It often contains persuasive advertisements urging the reader to come to a social in the parish hall, or to join in a treasure hunt on the hill, or to demonstrate community spirit by participating in a litter drive on the strand, all such notices carefully stressing that these events will provide excellent opportunities for neighbours to meet and increase their acquaintanceship. Such temptations I have always resisted with little difficulty. It has never been my idea of fun to spear crisp bags or rack my brain in the solution of improbable clues with a stranger who coincidentally has elected to live within a mile or so of my abode. I am not a neighbourly being, not in that sense.

Killiney means everything to me, nevertheless, for one reason, and that alone. It was in Killiney that I discovered my *métier*. My vocation. What I was born to do.

I am a dog-killer.

I did not choose this way of life deliberately. When I was of an age to select a career, I was too indecisive a character to be able to deliberately single out anything, even a biscuit from a plate containing three different kinds (I used to close my eyes and trust to luck, usually with disastrous results). I was, as the technical term has it, a drifter. I drifted from job to job, from activity to activity, a scrap of flotsam on the sea of life. If you could call the confined noisy hopeless office-world of Dublin a sea, or life. First I worked for the Corporation, which was a bit like working for the Russian civil service before the Revolution (or perhaps even after, but one doesn't know that experience so intimately). My duties consisted, for the most part, in writing addresses on envelopes, for the least, in dealing with telephone queries from a mystified but cantankerous public.

After a destructive eighteen months, I sacrificed my security and pension and studied electronics for a year, at a tech. Then I worked with a computer company for six months, until I was made redundant. Then I washed dishes in a German café in Capel Street, where, incidentally, I picked up a great deal of my employers' language as well as much other information which I have since found very useful. Then, at long last I got what I considered my great break. I was given a job as a folklore collector by a museum in Dublin. I was supplied with a tape-recorder and camera, and every day I walked around the city and environs ferreting out likely informants. When I had tracked them down, I interviewed them, interrogating them on a wide variety of topics loosely related to traditional belief and practice, with the aid of an easy-to-follow guide-book. It was a fascinating and rewarding task, entirely suited to my skills and disposition. It cultivated in me a taste for adventure, exploration and, above all, absolute freedom to order my days without deference to the will of an authoritative, pettifogging bureaucracy. These tastes, once realized, developed in strength and persistence, so that liberty soon became an imperative for survival as far as I was concerned. When my collecting job finished, as it did inevitably and all too soon, I was left nursing the burden of the knowledge that I could never again return to the slavery of a nine-to-five position, which indignity I had endured for seven long years before my break.

The question was, what should I do instead? Killiney gave me the answer. I had officially been resident there for two years before my collecting job collapsed. My enthusiasm for my work had been such, however, that I had hitherto paid little attention to my surroundings, frequently, indeed, not returning home at night, but bedding down in the flat of a colleague, or in the home of one of the friendly folk who provided me with the stuff of my occupation. But, even in that state of almost total apathy to environmental hazards, it had often struck me that Killiney suffered from unusually severe infestation by the canine species in all its varieties, too numerous to mention and in any case not known to me by name, except for some of the more common forms, such as Golden Labrador or Cocker Spaniel. I had once been bitten by a lean and hungry Alsatian belonging to some itinerants who camped, with my full approval (not that they asked for it, or required it) on an undeveloped site at the end of my lane. I had had to go to St Michael's for a tetanus injection, which had been administered by an aggressive nurse wearing steel-rimmed spectacles. On another occasion, a minute Pekinese, a breed which I particularly distrust, scraped the skin off the heel of an expensive shoe I had just purchased. Apart from these extreme incidents, every night that I spent in Killiney was filled with the mournful howling of dogs. Any walk taken in the neighbourhood was spoiled by the effort of fighting my fear of being bitten, of planning, futilely, itineraries which would take me out of the beasts' range, or of physically chasing off the ever-encroaching packs of curs.

When I had finished collecting folklore and had begun to live in Killiney almost constantly, it soon became apparent to me that the dog problem was rendering life unbearable; not only my life, but everyone else's as well.

My work as a folklore collector had not only awoken in me a healthy desire to master my own experience. It had imbued me with what can best be described as an altruistic streak. I wanted to improve the existence of others, too. In short, I was burning with ambition to be of service to mankind.

Killiney showed me the way.

My first dog-killing was fortuitous. I was walking home from the station one evening, having spent a particularly wearisome day trying to get a week's supply of food for four pounds, followed by an attempt to obtain an admission card to the National Library, where I had hoped to improve my mind with some classical reading while I considered my future. Both efforts had been fruitless. Lightly laden with two sliced pans, two tins of baked beans and a pound of liver, I had meandered up Kildare Street, the consciousness of impending starvation slowing my footsteps. My entrance to the Library was first blocked by a stern official in a blue suit, who accused me of trying to force entry without a reader's ticket, and thoroughly investigated the contents of my plastic bag. He suspected it of containing a bomb, he explained afterwards. He then directed me to the office of an even sterner official with startling blue hair who informed me in no uncertain terms that the National Library had no accommodation to spare for the likes of me. My pleas lasted the best part of an hour, but were all in vain. The more I reasoned, the stronger grew his opposition. Finally I left, strolling through the reading room on my way out. The porter in the hall did not check my bag, which I found convenient, since I had tucked into it the second volume of Plummer's *Lives of the Saints*, a work now exceedingly difficult to procure honestly but a handsome set of which adorned the library's open-access shelves. I resolved to return at my earliest opportunity to steal the remaining volumes, with the intention of making them available to an antiquarian bookseller just around the corner of Kildare Street.

I refreshed myself after the ordeal with a glass of lager in a nearby hotel, and then used my last fifty pence in the purchase of a ticket to Killiney Station. I was obliged to endure the journey in a vertical position, since I had stupidly elected to travel on the five-fifteen, the most crowded train in Ireland. My state of mind was, therefore, far from tranquil or positive when, halfway down Station Road, a dog, something like a collie but with a terrier's nose, dashed across my path and attempted to grab my raincoat in his mawful of bared teeth. I lowered my umbrella before you could say Jack Robinson and hammered him on the skull. To my intense relief he immediately released his vice-like grip and lay, subdued, at my toes. I stared at his immobile body for a moment or two, enjoying a vigorous sensation of triumph. I waited, patiently, for the beast to struggle to his paws and slink furtively away, tail demurely tucked between legs, aware of who was master. A minute passed and he did not stir. The smile which had played on my lips receded. Thirty more seconds elapsed. He continued to lie prostrate on the concrete path. Not a whimper passed his lips. I bent down and touched his hairy back, somewhat gingerly. It was warm to my fingers, but I felt uneasy. There was an unearthly stillness in the texture of the fur. I turned his head over and his eyes bored into mine. Round and lifeless, rolling in their sockets. Aghast, I sprang to my feet. The cooling lump of dog meat on the path was dead, and I had killed it! Never until that moment had I murdered a fly.

Fortunately, my keen instinct for survival warned me that there was no time to be lost in foolish lamenting over spilt milk. The immediate necessity was to dispose of the dog with maximum haste and secrecy. Observing that all was quiet on the road, not a soul in sight, I emptied my plastic bag of its contents and hid them under a bush. In their place I put the deceased animal, intending to carry him home and give him a decent funeral: I simply could not run the risk of being asked to financially compensate some distraught pet-owner. The dog appeared to be a valueless mongrel but you never know. Sometimes it is precisely the ugliest specimens who turn out to have pedigrees as long as your arm. I knew of a charming spot near the sewage-plant where my victim would rest in eternal peace, since no one, human or canine, ever ventured there, for obvious reasons.

I walked home from what I preferred to regard as the scene of the accident, and placed the victim on the kitchen floor. Then I returned to the black spot to collect my groceries. They, however, were not to be found. Some cruel villain had stolen them. There goes dindins for five days, I thought, glumly. How could I survive without food until dole day, a whole week off? Hunger reared its ugly head, not for the first time during my spell of unemployment.

Strolling homewards, I noticed torn slices of bread, scraps of bloodied butcher's paper, in short, the debris of my groceries, scattered at intervals along the road. About a hundred yards from where the tragedy had occurred a large ugly dog relaxed in the shadow of a tree, langorously devouring the last of the liver. Horrible brute! I thought, wishing I had my umbrella with me, in order to give him a well-deserved whack. But it had stopped raining and my weapon was in its teak stand in my little hall.

Back in the cottage, I sat in the living room and stared vacantly at Bray Head. It was black and awe-inspiring against the grey evening sky, but it afforded me no refreshment. My stomach rumbled, a dead dog lay on my kitchen floor awaiting burial, and, once again, rain bucketed forth from the heavens, preventing all action. I hadn't a single penny in my purse. After a dreary hour of staring, I went to bed, supping on a drink of water, the quality of which was far from high.

Morning dawned bright and sunny, lifting my spirits momentarily. My breakfast of stale oats and cold water effected a deterioration of mood, restoring me to a realization of my undesirable predicament. The eyes of the dog, clear blue, were wide open and seemed to follow every move I made. If I'd had two pennies I would have placed them on those Mona Lisa orbs and shut them for once and for all (it was a trick traditionally used in the preparation of the dead for burial, as my old friends in the Liberties had often told me). As I rinsed my bowl in the earthenware sink, it occurred to me, suddenly, like a bolt out of the sky, that I was not, after all, going to cart the heavy dog all the way down to the sewage plant, nervously avoiding encounters with morning strollers. I was not going to cart him anywhere at all. I was going to eat him.

In my work as a folklore collector, I had spent two months investigating a particular genre of tale known professionally as the modern legend. Modern legends are stories which concern strange or horrifying or hilariously amusing events, and circulate as the truth in contemporary society. An example is the story of the theatre tickets. A man finds that his car is missing from its usual parking place. He reports the theft to the police, but a day later the car has been returned. Pinned to the windscreen is a note of apology, and two tickets for a theatre show that night, as a token of amendment. The car owner and his wife use the tickets, and return at midnight to find that their house has been burgled. Another example is 'The Surprise Birthday Party'. A man wakes on his birthday to find that he has received no cards or greetings whatsoever. He goes to work and, at lunchtime, his secretary invites him to accompany her to her flat for lunch. He accepts the invitation with alacrity, and they proceed to her apartment. She leaves him in the living room and entering the bedroom, says she will be back in a minute. He uses the opportunity to undress, and is sitting on the sofa, completely naked, when the bedroom door bursts open and his wife, children, neighbours and colleagues leap into the room singing 'Happy Birthday to You'. In the course of my wanderings in Dublin I had learned that the best-known legend, amounting really to little more than belief, reported the use of dog as food in Chinese restaurants. Alsatian Kung Fu, Sweet and Sour Terrier, Collie Curry, were familiar names to me. It had taken only a trifle of investigation to discover that it was untrue that the Chinese served dog in their Irish outlets, but that in China and other parts of Asia, dog was consumed as a normal part of the diet.

I got out my carving-knife (my mother had given it to me as a house-warming present when I moved to the cottage: it is a long sharp knife with a bone handle, an antique, she told me) and flayed the animal. It was not easy, but neither was it as difficult as it may sound. In a matter of an hour or so the soft brown skin, dripping, it must be admitted, with soft wet blood, lay on a wad of newspaper on the floor. Then I sliced meat off the trunk of the dog: its legs were fragile and skinny and would be good for nothing but stock. Within half an hour, I had removed all edible flesh from the carcass (I had long ceased to think of it as a corpse). I carried the remains out to the yard and pondered how best to dispose of them. First I considered burning, but decided that the smell of roasting flesh might carry to my unknown neighbours and arouse anxiety among them. I secondly contemplated dumping them into the adjacent ocean. This thought developed rapidly into a better plan. I would walk to the sewage-plant where I had first considered burying the total animal, and throw what remained of him into the cesspool, which was open to the public. The body would be processed with the effluent from Shankill and whatever else went into the stinking hole, and leave no trace to be discovered, now or ever. The plan seemed so foolproof that I immediately felt happier than I had at any stage of my life since my terrible encounter with the keepers of the national literature some twenty hours earlier.

It worked like a dream. No one observed me as I plodded along the uncomfortable shingle towards the plant. No one observed me climb to the edge of the cesspool, and no one observed me tip the sack of bones into it. Coming home, sauntering along the tide line, now and then running out to avoid a brazen wave, I met a man leading a red setter, and bade him a cheery 'Good morning'. He smiled genially in response. No trace of knowledge or malice marked his weather-beaten countenance. I had been undetected.

I made a curry of the meat for Saturday's dinner: I had some spices in my cupboard, relics from more affluent days, as well as a cup of brown rice, which I prefer to the white: it is so much better for the digestion. The meal was superb: aromatic, tender, of a delicacy which I had never sampled before in the take-aways of Blackrock, Dun Laoghaire or even China, which I had visited as a student on a package trip. I had some leftover curry for Sunday's lunch (it tasted even better then) and two hefty cutlets for tea on the Sabbath. I had not eaten so well in several months.

The skin of the dog lay in my yard over the weekend. The blood dried off and the pelt seemed to be curing itself naturally. I cut off the straggly corners where the legs and tail protruded. I always hate those bits of animal skins, even on sheepskins. They seem so ostentatious. As if one were giving proof that the skin were real and not spun-nylon. I laid my genuine pelt in front of the fireplace. It looked shaggy, warm and inviting. I decided that I would refer to it in future conversations, even those which were conducted exclusively in my own company, (which accounted for most), as my antelope, received from a friend who hunted in Gambia, where, I vaguely recalled, antelope still survived in sufficient numbers to be hunted. My friend visited Africa every spring, I'd decided, when the antelope were small.

One thing led to another. My natural antipathy to the canine species, my diagnosis of Killiney's main problem as the dog problem, my urgent need for lucrative entrepreneurial employment, all conspired to persuade me that dog-killing would be my next job. I plunged into it with my whole heart. It was so easy, after all, to find prey. Indeed, it usually found me, snapping and yelping at my feet whenever I ventured out of the house. It was a simple matter to remember to carry my large umbrella, bought, in any case, as a weapon, and to batter any nosy beast on the head, on the right spot just above the temple (death was invariably instant and painless). I always carried a big shopping bag on my hunting expeditions, and suffered few setbacks in transporting carcasses from strand, street or railway to my home.

My methods of disposing of the products of my enterprise varied and expanded in variety as time passed. Initially basing my plans on the knowledge I had acquired as a folklore collector, I offered the flesh, neatly packaged in plastic cling-foil, to restaurants, at prices which were attractively but not suspiciously low. I did not, of course, approach Chinese or Indonesian restaurants. The owners would have immediately recognized my wares for what they were, and who knows what their reactions would be. Never trust a foreigner. No, I circulated the more exclusive native establishments, the cosy wee bistros with which the southern coastline of Dublin is so liberally peppered. I had, on the rare occasions when I had treated myself to a repast at 'The Spotted Dog' or 'The Pavlovian Rat', to name a couple of the better establishments, noted that they served food which was spiced and sauced to such a degree that its basic ingredients, no doubt of the best quality, were totally unrecognizable. They might as well have served *Rat à la Provencale*, or *Cat Bourguignon*, for all the evidence of veal or beef one could detect in either. The inhabitants of South Dublin, reared for the most part in primitive Ireland (i.e. not South Dublin), know nothing about food. All through their formative years they are fed on the Irish housekeeping tradition, and nothing else. Their mothers, bursting with pride about their home cooking, can concoct at best soda bread (the most tasteless, unhealthy bread imaginable), mixed grills, and boiled chicken. The natural reaction after such a diet is to crave the most elaborate messes of marjoram, tarragon, garlic, cream cheese, tomatoes, wine, ginger, and turmeric, all rolled into one cosmopolitan topping for pork masquerading as veal or monkfish doing duty for prawns. This taste is well catered for in every suburban village, if they can be called villages, those outcrops of shops and pubs and chapels which stud the concrete jungle from Bray to Booterstown. The northern Dubliner, at least while he stays on his own side of the river, probably still relies on his native cuisine, that is, coddle. I knew a man in the Corporation from Finglas West who always cooked coddle for lunch. He put it on at eleven o'clock at his teabreak and took it off at one, when it was done to a turn. He gave me a saucerful once. Delicious!

The reception I received at first from the proprietors and chefs of my local trattoria was not enthusiastic. It was on the whole suspicious. Where had I got the meat? Did I have identification? And so on.

It was not hard to procure an identity card. What is identification, after all? Just a card stating that you are who you claim to be. Having to create cards, however, prompted me to use several aliases, something which would never have occurred to me had I not been asked for identification in the first place.

As to explaining the provenance of the meat, I had, prior to my very first visit to the manager of a cosy kitchen in Dalkey, fabricated my story. The meat, I had decided was not antelope, but wild goat, imported from the North, where wild goats abound in the hills of Antrim and Tyrone. I had a partner in Crossmaglen who procured the meat for me from local lads, target-practising in the mountainy regions. It was tasty and healthy, perfect for Cordon Bleu cookery. Indeed, I added, Swiss chefs prized goats above any other viand. The belief that it was stringy and tough was ill-founded. I would give the restaurateur a sample batch, free, for testing.

This tale, in conjunction with the identity card, worked. It was the bit about the North which added the final touch of plausibility to my explanation. Anything could happen in the North, in the view of Dublin burghers. They had heard of smuggled TVs and refrigerators, smuggled pigs and cattle. Why not smuggled goat?

To cut a long story short, within six months I was regularly supplying twenty restaurants with dog meat and making a tidy profit. I continued to dump the denuded carcasses in the cesspool, but found that I was having a problem with the increasing heap of skins in my back yard: yellow, black, brown and red, they lay there in a multi-coloured pile. I had carpeted my living room with them, and very fine it looked, but I did not want my whole house covered with reminders of my trade, and, even had I wanted it, I would have encountered a problem sooner or later.

After much deliberation I decided to shave the dog skins and keep the hairs. The leftover skin I would, perhaps, at some future stage, sew into handbags, belts and other fancy leather goods. For the present, I contented myself with the purchase of forty yards of yellow cotton, and proceeded to make beanbags and cushions which I stuffed with dog hair. I opened a stall in a street market in town where I would not be recognized as the goat importer, and most Saturdays and Sundays I could be found there vending my wares to a receptive public: my products were cheaper, softer and more hard-wearing than anyone else's.

Time went on, as it does, and I became more and more comfortable financially, and more and more fulfilled as a human being. I developed my hunting technique, advancing from the simple umbrella to the more complicated sling, which, of course, had the advantage of being able to kill from a distance, and on to the even more complex pop-gun. I began to travel the length and breadth of Dublin, realizing that if I depleted the canine population of Killiney too much and too quickly someone would become anxious and interfere. As luck would have it, nobody at all seemed to notice what was happening, although the community benefited in no uncertain measure.

Good fortune is never limitless, and I was caught at last. It happened as I strolled along Dollymount Strand, pop-gun in pocket, car parked nearby, stalking a large English sheepdog. Normally I did not touch English sheepdogs or other expensive models with a ten-foot pole, but this one seemed to be very much alone. It had an abandoned look in its shaggy fringes and the lope of its melancholy feet spoke of endless deprivation. I felt it would be a kindness to take the animal out of its misery, and took a shot from a distance of fifty yards. The beast toppled and fell. Immediately, a man grabbed my shoulders. He was young, over six feet tall, and broad-shouldered. I did not struggle.

'I saw what you just did,' he said. He had an American accent and whined. 'You just shot my dawg!'

'Why, yes, I did,' I said.

'You can even stand there and admit it to my face!'

'Of course I can admit it. Why shouldn't I admit it? It was a complete mistake! Please accept my heartfelt apologies.'

'Aw! Sure it was a mistake! I saw you. You took aim and fired at him. My dawg!'

'I was trying to shoot that buoy over there,' I said, pointing at one of those plastery-looking life-savers in a wooden box which was, luckily enough, situated close to where the dog had fallen.

'I'm taking you to the police. Tell them your story if you like.'

He ushered me along the beach towards a Renault 12, red in colour, pausing on the way to examine the taxation disc on my windscreen. Then he drove rapidly down to the Bull Wall, across the bridge and to Clontarf barracks.

'You won't believe what I'm going to tell you,' he said to the sergeant, who was sitting beside a gas fire reading the *News of the World*.

'Well?' said the sergeant, with a great show of patience. His name, I noticed from a sign on the desk, was Sergeant Byrne. An unusual name for a Dublin guard.

'This broad here . . .' he indicated me with a flick of his shoulder '. . . shot my dawg.'

'What?' Sergeant Byrne looked up from his paper in some surprise.

'She shot my dawg. With a shotgun.'

'What is your name?' Sergeant Byrne asked me. I handed him one of my identity cards. *Imelda Byrne, 10 Dundela Park, Sandycove*, it stated.

'Do you have a gun licence?'

'No. It's a toy gun.'

'Let me see it.'

I showed him my pop-gun. It is a toy gun. It shoots wooden pellets. The trick is to aim at the temple.

'Well, well,' said the sergeant, 'and why did you shoot this man's dog?'

'It was a mistake. I was target-practising. I play golf, you see, and someone told me it would be good training for the eye to shoot at targets with a pop-gun.'

'I saw her aim at my dawg.'

'Yes, yes, well,' said the sergeant, 'we'll hold her for questioning. You can press charges, if you like. Fill in this and post it to us as soon as possible.' He handed the American a form.

The American departed, muttering under his breath. The sergeant sat, re-opened his paper and looked at me quizzically.

'Target-practising is an odd sport for a lady to carry out on a Sunday afternoon. Can't you find a healthier way of passing the time?'

'I usually play golf.'

'Oh, yes, yes. Where do you play?'

'Newlands.'

'Oh, yes, yes. Hard to get into these days, isn't it? I play a bit of golf myself, you know. Up at Howth, usually. Very hard to get into a good club.'

'Yes.'

'Hm. So you shot this dog, did you? Haha! Well, to tell you the truth, the more dogs get shot, the better life will be in this neighbourhood. I'm moidhered with them and with people's complaints about them. What can I do? I'm only human. Now, be off with you.'

I collected my car from the beach and drove home. It was a great relief to me to know that what my heart has always told me was true: right and might were on my side. I was fighting the good fight.

After my ordeal on Bull Island, I decided to relax for at least one evening. Normally my Sunday nights were absorbed in account-keeping, doing the books, as the phrase has it, for the week. But on this particular Sunday I lit a fire in the drawing room and settled down to watch a video: I had a complete set of Bergman movies that I had not watched before. I adore Bergman. The film I selected was *Face to Face*, a slow-moving study of a psychiatrist and her rela-tionship with her daughter, patients, husband, lovers, and others. I was just getting involved in it when my door-knocker sounded. A rare, almost unique, occurrence. I smelt danger immediately but had no option but to open it, since the blue glow of my living room would have indicated to anyone that I was in, glued to the box. At the door were two policemen, who asked me if I was Jane O'Toole. Shocked, I admitted that I was. They produced a warrant for my arrest.

I got six months. The judge said it was as much as he could impose although he heartily wished he could condemn me to a life of hard labour. My offence, he said, in a long tedious monologue at the end of my three-day trial, was the most heinous he had encountered in his life. I had been responsible, he said, for the killing of at least a thousand dogs (in fact, twice that). Responsible dogs. The beloved pets of the citizens of Dublin.

Now I am sitting in Mountjoy in the female wing, engaged in writing an autobiographical novel. Public sympathy for my crusade against the dogs is expressed by a flood of letters from people who have, in one way or another, been molested by them. Even the warders, a tough and unemotional crew, express concern for the fact that several hundred dogs roam the area within half a mile radius of the prison and threaten them every time they leave for a walk or to go home.

I am comfortable in prison and happy with the degree of free-dom which I am allowed. I do not have to work and the only constraints are physical: I am not allowed outside the high walls which surround the penitentiary. Inside, I may do as I wish. I am not as happy as I was when enjoying my career as a dog-killer, but I am happier than I have been in many of my other jobs. I find fulfilment of a kind in writing down my account of my life's experiences and struggle for freedom. More than one publisher has expressed interest in my project, which has already received considerable publicity in the media. According to some agents, I stand to score a huge success with the book. It will, they explain, be a matter of 'hype', and already it has been hyped to a much greater extent than any author could wish, and all for free. I could, taking into account the possibilities of film rights, translations, and so on, make at least a hundred thousand. And it will, like all my previous profits, be tax-free.

12

PEACOCKS

The park is called El Parque de Isabel La Catolica. It is at the east end of the promenade, and boasts a rose arbour, a bowling green, and an outdoor café. Also dozens of peacocks, walking or strutting about, sometimes displaying their tails and sometimes concealed in the treetops, screaming like demented souls about to suffer eternal damnation.

It is to see these peacocks that Anita has brought her daugher, Aisling, here.

'Look!' she cries, as one of the birds emerges from the pink shadow of some rose bushes and crosses their path. His tail is closed but even so Anita finds the very appearance, the very existence of these splendid birds, in such numbers, and so freely visible, exciting and pleasurable. She has encountered peacocks frequently, of course, but usually meagrely apportioned, one or two at a time, in the garden of some old big house or castle, the kind that has ceased to be a home and is now on display to the public at ten pounds a tour, coffee and carrot cake in the stables an optional extra. It is the abundance of the birds that elates her now as much as the beauty of their tails. 'Look, how splendid!' she repeats. Anita is a woman lately given to repetition and to excitement. These days she behaves as if she lived in a constant state of elation; she expostulates from morning to night.

Anita, her partner Marcus, and Aisling, her daughter, have come to Spain for a few weeks. It is what Anita terms an 'unstructured trip', meaning they haven't booked most of their accommodation in advance, an idea which was more pleasurable in the anticipation than the practice. The plan is that they will travel around, perhaps by train or perhaps in a rented car, stopping whenever the humour takes them. But already they have stayed put for four days in Madrid, days during which Aisling remained in her hotel room while Marcus and Anita nervously visited the principal tourist spots, dashing through the vast galleries, museums and department stores, always rushing back to the hotel to make sure Aisling was 'alright': to make sure, in fact, that she had not run away and lost herself irretrievably and deliberately somewhere in the mysterious city. After that less than relaxing introduction, they came north by train to this resort on the Bay of Biscay where Anita had spent a summer once, as a student, working as a chambermaid in one of the seafront hotels and practising her Spanish. For three days they have been based here. Already more than a week of their fortnight has elapsed and they have stayed in only two places. The vision of eneregetic touring, a new town every day, has already evaporated. Anita blames Aisling. She is not in the mood for travelling, or seeing a lot of strange places. But the truth is that Anita herself is showing a propensity to nest. This tendency is more apparent here in the north than it was in Madrid.

She has her memories. Maybe that is it. They are staying in the hotel in which Anita had stayed before, when she was a teenager, but under such different circumstances. She enjoys the sense of tables having turned, indulges in the interesting sensation of being master where once she was, literally, maid. It is a lush and splendid place, this hotel, located in an old manor house on the edge of the town. One night in a magnificent room, draped with velvet curtains, furnished in the simple, upright, darkly magnificent traditional style, for Anita and Marcus, and a smaller but equally luxurious room for Aisling, cost as much as four nights in the small modern hotel in which they had lodged in Madrid. It is worth it, Anita feels, and not only for its nostalgic associations. Aisling actually likes it. The subtle luxury and mellow grandeur had impressed her, had awoken her, at least briefly, from the dream in which she has immersed herself for most of the trip. She had smiled when she walked into the lobby, lush with palm trees in pots, with the wink of brass and polish. She had turned to Anita and said in a wondering voice 'Did you really work here?'

It seemed to Anita that that was the first time she had smiled in five days, or made a spontaneous comment. It was the first time she had pulled aside the veil which separated her from the ordinary world, and especially from her mother.

'Yes I did!' Anita said in the sparkling cheery tone which has become customary with her ever since Aisling became anorexic and moody. In the past, she has been as prone to gloom as anyone else. But now that she is worried about Aisling she takes care not to indulge her own dark feelings. In fact she seldom has any, or not for more than half an hour. It is as if her tendency to dramatize has moved offstage, to make way for Aisling's. Or maybe it is simpler than that. Maybe there is just so much gloom one household can contain, unless it is prepared to spill over into madness. Anita and Marcus have ceased to be the central players and have become bulwarks against the encroaching terror, they who were not so long ago prone to experience and display the full spectrum of emotions, in all their barbarity and pointlessness.

The hotel is at the opposite end of town from the park, at the west end of the magnificent beach with its gay flutter of sunbathers, its outsize Atlantic breakers dashing against the sand. Anita and Aisling have walked the promenade behind this beach to get to the park, a walk taking about half an hour. Now they have seen the peacocks. What else is there to do, to offer Aisling?

A Diet Coke?

'No thanks,' she mutters, her blue eyes shifting. 'Can we go back to the hotel now?'

This has been her most frequent request since she came on holiday.

Anita was nineteen when she visited Spain, the same age that Aisling is now. But she was in a very different position: a lone student coming to take up a low-paying job rather than a daughter accompanied by cosseting parents. She had got the job in this little-known resort through the student's union in Dublin, and travelled laboriously, by boat and train, all the way to Asturias. She had had very little money, and could not afford to eat in restaurants or cafés, but had had to buy bread and bottled water at railway station kiosks and make do with that. When she had found that she could not get from Calais to Spain in one day, but would have to stay overnight in

Bordeaux, panic had set in because her budget did not include any money at all for overnight accommodation. Although she was nineteen she had never been abroad before in her life. Suddenly she was faced with an array of challenges: the boat, the strange trains, the foreign accents and then the foreign languages; and now the challenge of finding a place to stay, cheap enough for her tiny budget. Her parents had not realized how long the journey was, or that she might need an emergency fund. She had ten pounds, which was all she had left over from her Saturday job, where she earned a pound for working in a sweetshop, plus some free sweets. But she had found a room, helped by a medical student she met on the train, who tried to persuade her to share his flat with him (she resisted the temptation, although he offered plenty of blandishments: she would have her own room with her own key; he would give her dinner. And plenty of threats: the only hotel she would afford would be full of prostitutes. A girl had been beheaded there a week ago. Beheaded? Yes, they found her head in the bath and her body on the floor of her room). Anita was so short of cash and so full of fear and idealism that she had almost succumbed, but some basic sense of self-preservation had stepped in and saved her from whatever fate might have been in store. And still she could remember her mixed feelings, as she lay in her horrible room, the size of a toilet, and listened to the footsteps walking the corridors all night – he was probably right about the prostitutes. She had felt that she had been prudish. She berated herself for not being brave enough to accept the offer of help, for who knows what friendships, what new experiences, it could have led to? But she had not, and the next morning at 6 a.m. she was at the bus station, with enough money to buy her ticket to Spain and one cup of coffee. The medical student was there too, to say hello and carry her bags to the bus, convincing her that she had misjudged him.

She arrived at the hotel ten hours later, hungry and exhausted. The housekeeper, Maria, a grey-haired woman with dark skin and a sweet smile which belied her despotic character, installed her in a hut at the bottom of the hotel garden, where all the summer staff lived in a row of shacks resembling accommodation for slaves on a cotton plantation. The hut was very small, containing two bunk beds, a wardrobe and a chair. There was space to stand between the bunks and the wall, but even so it would have to be shared with someone else, who had not arrived as yet. This was early June. The summer season was just beginning. For Anita it was to be a season of narrow quarters but expansive experiences. 'You can eat dinner at midnight,' Maria announced. 'Did you say midnight?' Anita thought she had misunderstood Maria's rapid Spanish. But no: the staff ate when the hotel guests had finished their meal, and dinnertime in Spain is ten o'clock, even for people who do not work in hotels. She spoke with an authority that brooked no resistance. Anita had travelled for three days, and was dropping dead from exhaustion, but this did not seem to occur to Maria. All she saw in front of her was a chambermaid, a machine which would start cleaning bedrooms tomorrow at eight, a different species from the hotel guests, who were encouraged to be tired after their journeys, to need sustenance at any time of the day or night, to expect friendly solicitations, motherly care. Anita realized, if she had not suspected it as she made her laborious way south, that she had moved into a shadowland, where nobody cared about her wellbeing. It provided an interesting contrast to home, where in general people cared too much. But once she was away from her mother, she was finding out that only a lot of money would buy anything approaching the material attention that irked her so terribly as a rule.

That evening she skipped dinner, and survived on the breakfast of greasy doughnuts and coffee until lunch next day – 4 p.m. for staff. Missing meals, anyway, was something she still counted as a bonus. At home her mother was constantly pushing food on her, food which she rejected as often as not, in the interests of getting even thinner than she already was. This attitude was destined to change as the summer wore on and tables turned. But now at the start of the holiday she still retained the habits she had indulged in as a student in Dublin. Maria's lack of even superficial polite interest in her wellbeing she found shocking, but she was still pleased to take advantage of it. She calculated a loss of two or three pounds over the first days of the trip, meaning she would have a bit of leeway for her first week. Life consisted of a balancing act, a calculation of weight loss and weight gain. She was on the verge of anorexia, though she did not know the word. Pounds lost were money in the bank, and she loved to watch the negatives mount up, like a miser counting his ducats.

'It's time for lunch!' announces Anita, luxuriously. Anita is now an overweight woman approaching forty, with a double, nay treble, chin and bright blonde hair, neatly clipped. She wears outsize ear-rings and large rings on every finger, perhaps to distract attention from the rings around her neck. She knows she is too fat to be graceful, which is what she originally specialized in, and is aiming instead at a chunky sexiness. Her clothes are simple, skimpy and expensive.

She is sitting with Marcus and Aisling in the big dark-red bed-room. Marcus is lying on the four-poster bed, reading. Aisling is fiddling with the television remote control. 'Let's go!'

'Aaah!' Aisling groans and grimaces.

'I really think you should eat something,' says Anita, hearing her own mother's tone in her voice. 'You had nothing for breakfast.'

'Yeah, but I'm not really hungry,' says Aisling, who is openly and, it seems to Anita, stubbornly, anorexic and has been seeing a coun-sellor every week for the past two years, to no avail whatsoever. 'Why don't you buy me some fruit and water and bring it back to the hotel for me later?'

Marcus closes his book with a slight snap, jumps quickly off the bed and gets his linen jacket from the wardrobe.

'Fine, let's go!' he says decisively.

Anita gets the stab of panic she always feels when she has to let Aisling out of her sight.

'See you later,' says Aisling, glumly but firmly, a personal style that has evolved over some years of dealing with her mother's protec-tiveness.

'OK!' Anita sings in her upbeat sing-song. Smiling in what she trusts is an uplifting, careless way, a way which will provoke feelings of independence and love, not guilt and worry, she leads Marcus out of the room.

'You can't force her,' says Marcus, as they examine the menu. They are sitting at a table on a terrace overlooking the harbour outside an old grey stone restaurant. Already they have a glass of red wine, glit-tering in the sunshine. The sun sparkles on the sea, glints off the chrome of yachts and boats. The menu is a poem of prawns and crabs and lobsters and a dozen kinds of exotic fish.

'I know,' sighs Anita. 'But I wish she could you know, get something out of all of this. Enjoy it.'

'That's up to her,' says Marcus, who has consistently been more pragmatic in his approach to Aisling and her problems, recognizing the limits of his influence. 'We can't enjoy it for her. The least we can do is try to enjoy it ourselves.' He sits back and observes a waiter pour a glass of cider for a diner at the next table, where four young men are sitting. The waiter holds the bottle high above his head, and the glass as far below as he can reach. The cider spills from the bottle like a waterfall and cascades into the glass beneath. Some splatters the floor. It's the traditional method of pouring the traditional cider in this region, something to do with making it fizz. Some of the waiters perform the operation in a workmanlike, functional way, quickly raising the bottle and lowering the glass, pouring with the grim attitude of weight-lifters. Others, like this one, do it with flamboyance, showing off. The cider isn't actually all that nice, Anita has tried it. But the young men are enjoying the pouring and the beverage to the full. They swallow the drink quickly, in one draught, as they are supposed to, and laughingly encourage the waiter to further gymnastic efforts. Anita finds herself wishing that Aisling were here watching the fun. Maybe she would manage to get talking to these bright, happy young people, make a friend? Aisling has never had a boyfriend, to Anita's knowledge, although she is nineteen and a half. All her dieting has led to nothing romantic, even though she is very pretty as well as very thin. It seems that her attention is too focused on her own body, specifically on her own weight, to admit love, or romance, or even flirtation. She is a virgin serving at the altar of skinniness.

Anita orders scallops and asparagus, and sips her wine. Gradually she puts her daughter to the back of her mind. She begins to enjoy the drink, the food, the view. She loves Spain, as she always loves every new country, savouring everything about it that is different from home, beautiful, exotic. She is an enthusiastic tourist, and always has been, since her first exhilarating visit to this place. That Aisling seems to feel absolutely none of the thrill of travelling disappoints her. She has failed to transfer to her daughter the capacity for wonder at new things which she possessed in enormous abundance at her age: just one more maternal failure.

'It's nothing to do with you,' says Marcus, who is given to quick judgements and possesses a lot of common sense. 'A, she's on holiday with her mother, not a situation calculated to inspire any teenager to feelings of wonder. And B, she's been abroad dozens of times, since she was a year old. She's spoiled.' He pauses and adds, 'Just like most people of her age. They take all this sort of thing for granted.'

'Not dozens of times,' says Anita. But more than half a dozen. Maybe nine or ten trips. Naturally the edge has been taken off the experience because she was experiencing it before she knew what was going on. Planes and boats and trains are everyday affairs for her. 'Through a chink too wide there comes in no wonder,' Patrick Kavanagh wrote, Anita thinks. Anyway, whoever wrote it, it is a line that often passes through her mind. For Anita a plane, first experienced when she was in her twenties, was a magic carpet. How could it have the same effect on someone who went to New York to do the Christmas shopping when she was four, even if it was courtesy of a Superquinn voucher?

'Too often,' says Marcus. 'Jennifer is just the same.'

Jennifer is his own daughter, by his first wife. Jennifer is three years younger than Aisling and lives with her mother, and seems incredibly well adjusted. She is happy as a clam. Her mother is not as much happy as sensible. Authoritative, sure of herself, nasty as hell to Marcus and Anita. Her voice on the phone, if Anita ever picks it up when she is contacting Marcus to discuss something concerning their child (i.e. to ask him for money) is chilly as a dead hand, and as business-like as a bank manager's, which in fact is what she is. But Anita admires her for it. Assertive is what she is, so assertive that Marcus left her, she sometimes adds, meanly. She even has an assertive name: Pat. Not Patricia, not Patsy, not funny Paddy. Just Pat. 'This is Pat Lister,' she says, when Anita answers the phone. She does not say 'Hello,' even. She will not be tricked into giving Anita the time of day. Jennifer – never Jenny – is clever, got ten As in her Junior Cert, plans to study medicine at Trinity. Her life is already mapped out. She will follow the designated plan, a plan designed by herself, allegedly without any input from her assertive mother or practical father. Unlike Aisling. Aisling has already dropped out of her first year as a student of modern languages, and is now enrolled at an art college. Aisling would never dream of making a life plan. She has absolutely no idea what she wants to do later. In fact she does not seem to believe that there is 'later', as far as she is concerned, and the prospect of earning a living is not one she contemplates. If she considers the future at all, it is a vague dark forest, which she would just as soon not penetrate. She's certainly not making plans for what she will do in the unlikely event of getting there.

The sun dances on the harbour, the holidaymakers walk past, swinging their straw bags. The waiters stretch their arms like Swedish gymnasts and pour their cider. Anita feels happier, as the wine in the pitcher diminishes. Marcus's point, that she has to stop worrying about Aisling, and trying to rescue her from whatever depth of pain she has chosen to descend to, makes sense. 'I've done what I can,' she says, to herself. 'I've got to let go now.' She imagines letting go, floating away from Aisling into her own space, the space she always believed would be hers when Aisling grew up. Freedom, the space is called. Lightness of being.

Over the harbour white seagulls glide. Anita closes her eyes. She sees dozens of giant white balloons, snowy, silky, floating in the sky. The vision is so appealing that she wants to drift off, float into a state of airy unmotherliness, a blissful stratosphere where umbilical cords remain broken, where mothers and daughters and sons circle around one another, independent as angels.

'Are you falling asleep?' Marcus glances at her. She opens her eyes and the balloons disappear. Marcus returns to his phrase book. He's an engineer who likes to read in as many European languages as he can half master (so far, French, Italian, German, Danish, Dutch). By the time the two weeks are over he will have made considerable headway in Spanish, and will try to follow it up, polish it off, during the winter, maybe taking a course at some night school. Watching his stocky body, his big head bent over his book, his thick bushy grey hair springing up off his forehead, she feels a bolt of attraction, or a wish to reach into him. Marcus left his wife for her; he made that momentous move, upsetting his own routines and others', to move in with Anita, a single parent. That was proof of the strength of his passion. And initially their relationship was characterized by powerful love, true love, the love which cast a rosy glow over every aspect of life, which imbued it with a crystalline meaning. For this love, Anita had felt, human beings were created. It was the centre of the experience of living, Nirvana, and if you got it once, as she had, it would cast its benign light forward and backwards on every facet of your experience.

That is just as well, because the ecstasy of the affair has long fizzled away. For years Marcus has been gently withdrawing from the state of union, regaining his own territory, from which Anita is firmly excluded. And as he has pulled away, her goal has been to once again break down and through the barrier that separates them. Her goal has been to get to know him, heart and soul. Impossible. She knows it but it doesn't stop her trying.

She puts out a hand, and covers one of his with it. He stops reading and looks at her. A romantic moment is nipped in the bud, however, because at the crucial moment a fuss takes place at the next table. The four young men have just ordered coffee. The waiter has gone back into the bar to get it. There is ice cream on the table on a small silver dish, and glasses and a bottle of cider. Suddenly all four men jump up and dash across the terrace, knocking down a chair en route. They jump over the low wall at the edge of the terrace. By then a few people are shouting. The waiter re-emerges from the bar, a tray of coffee in his hand. His face drops, like the face of a character in a cartoon. Such shock! He goes to the table, looks at it and shakes his head. Then he shrugs, smiles and goes back into the bar.

After a few days at the hotel, the person Anita was to share her hut with arrived. She was lying on the top bunk when Anita came in from work, smoking and blowing rings into the air. The hut was filled with blue smoke.

'Hello there,' she said, in a loud voice, with what sounded to Anita like an English accent. She leaned over the edge of the bunk and looked down. 'I'm Sharon, from Swansea.' 'I'm Anita, from Cork,' said Anita, coughing and rubbing her eyes. Sharon was stout and sturdy, with a foxy hairstyle, streaked blond and brown. 'I'm sharing with you, it seems,' said Sharon, putting out her cigarette. 'I can see what it's like down here, but what about up there in the big house?' Anita considered Maria, sweet-looking and eagle-eyed, always pushing her to take on extra work. She thought of the ten cluttered rooms she had to clean every day, and of meals eaten at odd hours in the little dirty scullery. 'It's OK,' she said. 'You get used to it.'

'Yeah, I bet,' said Sharon. 'That Maria looks like a proper bitch an' all.' She jumped from the bunk, landing with a bang on the floor. The hut shook from the impact. 'Hope Uncle Tom's cabin don't collapse,' said Sharon. She was very plump, dressed in the shortest miniskirt and tight vest top. Her flesh bulged frankly over the rims of these clothes. Her thighs were large and flabby, and her feet stuffed into tiny high-heeled sandals. Anita had never known anyone quite like her. This was a time when Anita, thin, not tall, with wide green eyes and long brown hair straight as a plank, wore floating skirts and peasant blouses, the more to enhance her waifish appearance. Her favourite and most typical garment was a dress of snow-white cotton, smocked in white thread at the breast (of which she possessed none), and loose, that hung to her feet, and she liked to wear it with brown wooden beads strung around her neck, and flat sandals.

Sharon was a professional hotel maid, sent by some agency for catering staff based in Bristol. She had been working since she was fifteen and had, as she said, travelled the world, or at least the south of Europe, mop in hand. Maria and the owners of the hotel hoped she would spend the winter here, and she was paid almost twice as much as Anita to do the same work, to Anita's annoyance. They soon realized that they had as little in common as their different tastes in clothes indicated. But they were both nineteen. They shared a backbreaking job and a garden shed. They became good friends.

A routine established itself fairly quickly. When work and staff lunch were over, at about five in the afternoon, Sharon and Anita hit the beach, where they tanned themselves mercilessly until seven. Then they withdrew to the café in the park of Isabel the Catholic and sat there, drinking the cheap wine and preening themselves. Afterwards, they strolled along the prom, or through the fashionable shopping street which in the hours between five and ten became transformed to a great open air café and stage for those who liked to walk and show off their clothes and their bodies.

They first encountered Juan in the park. He came and sat at their table, and hit it off with Sharon from the start. He stared lustily at her large bosom, barely covered in orange cotton, with plenty of cleavage showing, and at her large legs emerging from white satin shorts. She was always going to make a more striking visual impact than Anita. Also she talked more, albeit in pidgin Spanish spoken with her indelible Welsh accent. That didn't bother Juan. He was a fair-haired, golden-skinned Spaniard, with the neat, almost effeminate features which often accompanied that colouring. He had one surprising feature, intensely bright blue eyes, unusual in Spain and of a colour not usual anywhere then, the kind of bright colour one nowadays associates with coloured contact lenses. But in spite of these eyes and his fair complexion he was as expressive and flamboyant as any southern stereotype. He spoke at high speed about his background, his job, his reason for being in the town, waving his arms, making funny faces, turning his perfectly ordinary life into the stuff of high drama. He didn't care that half of what he said was incomprehensible to Sharon; his motive was to perform, not communicate. Alcohol was not a factor, either; his favourite drink was coffee, and that is what he was drinking now. After the coffee he invited the girls to dinner, which they ate in a cider bar in the town centre. Then he and Sharon rambled off into the narrow, fish-scented streets at the end of the harbour while Anita found her way back to the hut.

Sharon came in at 5 a.m. Anita heard her – it would have been difficult to avoid this, given the confines of the hut – and glanced at the alarm, which she could barely make out in the dimness. But the sun was beginning to rise and there was a faint streak of light making its way into the hut through the one window. She pretended to be asleep when Sharon said 'Sorry, old woman!' An hour later Anita was springing out of bed, to the ring of the alarm, and up to the hotel to make early-morning coffee for the more energetic or insomniac guests.

Sharon conducted a relationship with Juan that was time-demanding but not very serious. 'He's a nice slab of meat,' said Sharon. 'But I can't understand a word the bleedin' man says.' Or she said 'He's a mummy's boy. His mother's on holiday with him, they have a house outside the town. Did you ever!' In spite of these reservations, she continued to see him every night and stay out till all hours. Her plump brown face developed rings under the eyes and she tended to be cross during the day, stomping around the bedrooms, yanking sheets off beds and dumping them angrily in the plastic tubs for the wash. Maria told her off frequently but Sharon shrugged and said 'Fuck off, you old bitch,' to her face. Maria did not understand a word of English.

'You need a good night's sleep,' Anita said, with more solicitousness than she felt. She was well rested herself. Too well rested. Now that Sharon was occupied with Juan, she had nobody to go out with. After lunch, instead of heading off to the cafés, she took to going for long walks up and down the promenade, or to the park. The walks, she reckoned, helped counteract the effect of the food she was eating, too much food, much more than she had ever eaten at home. There were no scales available but she knew she had put on pounds, she could feel a layer of flesh developing on her ribcage, on her waist, where before there had been skin and bone. It was a worry to her, but she needed the food in order to do the heavy work of the hotel. Being anorexic, she was discovering, was a luxury a chambermaid could not afford.

The loss of sleep told more and more heavily on Sharon. She yawned from morning to evening. Once, Maria caught her fast asleep on a double bed at eleven o'clock in the morning, and threatened to sack her. 'Fuck off you old bitch, you won't get another chambermaid at your rates in the middle of July,' said Sharon, stretching and planning to take a nap every day, if she could recruit Anita to guard her. To her she muttered darkly 'It's all right for him, he can sleep all day,' she grumbled. 'I need me beauty sleep.' It was all too true. Her beauty was suffering badly, and she was as haggard as somebody weighing twelve stone can be. Anita advised her to take a night off, off Juan. Reluctantly – 'I wouldn't trust that fella even for a night' – Sharon agreed. It was a Monday night, the last week of July, that Sharon selected for her rest cure, judging that after the excitement of the weekend, Juan might like some time off himself. 'Not him,' Sharon sighed in an exaggerated way, pleased that she was indispensable. 'He was right annoyed when I told him I wouldn't be out tonight. But if I don't get some sleep I'll go bleedin' barmy.'

'He knows that. And absence makes the heart grow fonder,' Anita muttered.

'It's not his heart I'm worried about,' said Sharon, a statement which Anita understood to be suggestively obscene but the implications of which she did not fully grasp.

She set off on her daily five-mile trek.

She was resting at the café in the park when Juan found her. Anita wished that she was wearing her one short skirt. But she had opted for her long white dress today, and looked like a Brontë orphan. Nevertheless Juan seemed pleased to see her and sat down, ordering the same drink she had, a mineral water.

He told her about Isabel La Catolica famous for her ruthless Catholicism and role in the Inquisition. He told her about the history of the town. In this town, the Moors had been first vanquished and their rule in Spain challenged by a king, King Pelayo. There was a statue of him close to the harbour, had she noticed it? Yes she had actually, although she could not recall the name. And he told her other things, about the history of the town. How it had been razed to the ground during the civil war, and had always been radical and left wing, due to the mining and industrial community which formed its core citizenship.

He told her all this with his usual histrionic skill, imbuing the story of the town with magic. But it was the fact that he knew some elementary historical facts that impressed Anita. She had assumed he hadn't a thought in his head. How could he care for someone like Sharon?

They walked through the grass, and watched the two peacocks who lived in a wired-in enclosure next to the rose arbour. The birds were skulking in a corner; they manifested their pride with sulks rather than display. But Juan whistled in a strange way and to Anita's surprise managed to draw one of the birds out of its seclusion. He came up to the wire and spread his magnificent tail for their pleasure. Juan slipped him a handful of peanuts. This also surprised Anita. She had somehow imagined that peacocks would eat special food, different from that of other birds, but this one was quite happy to gobble up the peanuts.

When Juan asked her to dinner, it seemed natural to accept the invitation.

Sharon never accused Anita of stealing her boyfriend. The theft occurred gradually. For a few weeks, Juan courted both chambermaids, his technique being to offer Sharon more and more nights off for 'her beauty sleep'. Then came the week when Anita saw Juan every evening, while Sharon stayed at home or went out with other girls from the hotel. By then Anita was too enamoured to think straight. Sharon discovered her strolling along the beach with Juan one evening. She acted with great presence of mind, greeting the pair without the slightest demonstration of surprise. Anita anticipated a confrontation when she returned to Uncle Tom's cabin. She foresaw fisticuffs, she wouldn't have been surprised if Sharon had beaten her up. But not a word was said.

Sharon simply stopped talking to her.

From then on, the atmosphere in the hut wasn't very comfortable, but Anita wasn't there much anyway. All her spare time was now taken up with Juan, who demanded of her the same attention and time he had got from Sharon. Anita was somewhat more protective of her sleep than Sharon had been, but even so she was seldom in bed before 2 a.m., more often 3.

They drank, they ate, they walked on the beach, they went for midnight swims. They went to the park and lay on the grass, under the bushes, kissing and pressing their bodies together. No sex, explicitly – Anita didn't do it then, it was that period when girls like her did not. And Juan seemed to understand her scruples at least for a few weeks.

When Marcus and Anita get back to the hotel, carrying plastic bags full of fruit and other provisions, Aisling is not there.

'She's probably just gone for a walk. Don't start worrying,' Marcus warns, straightaway. He pulls Anita down on the bed and kisses her. The wine and sun have made him affectionate.

She pulls away as soon as she can, unable to participate, her mind focused on Aisling. The feeling of freedom, the air balloons, are quite deflated.

'I'm going for a walk,' she says.

'You won't find her,' says Marcus. 'And you shouldn't. She'll be all right.'

'I'm afraid . . .' She does not voice her fear, which is that Aisling will do herself in. She will jump off the high wall of the pier into the sea, or find some other horrendous way of killing herself. This is why she is on tenterhooks from morning till night, watching Aisling like a personal bodyguard. She tries to let go but it is not easy. Aisling is anorexic, Aisling is unpredictable, Aisling has stopped being the carefree girl she was a year or two ago and has become her own worst enemy.

'You've done what you can. You do what you can. You can't tie her to you, like a baby.'

'Tie her to me? I don't want to do that. I want to let her go but she's in such a state I can't.' Anita believes this.

'Listen, Anita. Aisling is in danger, from her moods. But if it were not that she'd be in danger from something else: from driving around with some idiot young fella, from drink and drugs, from anything. You'd be trying to protect her from those things too. But you can't.'

'It's different,' says Anita. 'I mean if she were on drugs, I'd be worried. Yes. But if she were just out there, having a good time, living life to the full, I'd know she was always at risk of drugs or AIDs or whatever but I'd let her take the risk.' She thinks about it. 'Now she's not just at normal risk. She's there, in trouble. It's like she already had AIDs.'

'Yeah, well, even if she had, what could you do about it?'

Anita has no answer to this. She sits down on the silk sofa for a few minutes and thumbs through a newspaper. But she can't concentrate on it, and a few minutes later jumps up and says, 'I'm going for a walk to the park.'

Sharon did not speak to Anita for the rest of the summer. A few times Anita tried to break the silence. Sharon responded by turning her back and marching off, an action which she was able to perform with great panache, thanks to her sturdy build as much as her unassailable self-assurance. The first time she did it, she reduced Anita to tears. The second time, Anita felt depressed for a day. The third time, she shrugged and laughed.

Juan's knowledge of Spanish history was limited to five facts, all of which he had relayed to Anita on their first encounter alone. His interest in cultural matters in general was similarly confined. What absorbed him was football. Otherwise he busied himself keeping well-dressed, well-groomed, and in good physical shape. Every morning he spent two hours in an institution known as Charlie Gym, an exercise which he followed with a trawl through the shops of the town, often picking up a shirt or other garment in the course of his travels. He favoured dark colours, navy being a particular favourite, but always enlivened by a splash of some brilliant orange or red or white.

Anita found herself bored by his conversation after two weeks, but simultaneously more and more attracted to him. She thought about him all the time: his hair, his blue eyes, his thin, wiry arms. She did not believe that she lusted after his body, exclusively. It seemed to her that she loved him, whole and entire, body and soul, but it was his body she thought about, and his soul she would have found difficult to define. As far as personality was concerned, he was considerate in overt ways, holding the door, paying the bills. He listened to what she had to say, initially, but soon tired of that. She could not even say that he had that trump card of men, that he was 'a good listener'. In fact he was a terrible listener. But of course he found it difficult to understand her Spanish.

Her summer rolled on, combination of hard work which she found not unsatisfying, and time with Juan, on the beach, in the town. Her tan deepened to a dark brown, she put on a layer of sub-cutaneous fat. Her Spanish became fluent and her tendency to anorexia disappeared, cured by that most potent medication: love and work.

In the middle of August, Sharon disappeared without warning from the hotel. With her she took all Anita's money, and most of her clothes and personal belongings, even though they wouldn't possibly fit her. On the small unframed mirror which they had bought for the hut, she had scrawled in crimson lipstick 'Fucking Bitch'. Her handwriting was small and neat. Anita left the inscription there for the rest of the stay in Spain, for old time's sake.

Coincidentally, this happened the same weekend that Juan, and his mother, whom Anita had never seen, left their summer house and returned home to Madrid. He gave Anita his phone number and encouraged her to telephone if she ever was in the capital, and she planned to go home that way, flying. But after the robbery that became impossible. She had to use her last pesetas to telephone Cork, and ask for money for her fare, money from which her indigent and cautious mother was very reluctant to part with. However, after some persuasion she sent the necessary sum, and Anita went home. It had been a profitable summer. She had lost her virginity, her money and her clothes. But she had gained independence, love and excellent Spanish. She was no longer on the verge of anorexia, and never would be again.

Anita takes a taxi instead of walking to the park. She wants to get there quickly. Some instinct tells her that that is where she will find her daughter. The instinct is grounded in the awareness that Aisling has been to hardly any other place in the town, most of her time having been spent in her hotel room.

The park is quiet and green, as always. Along the paths, men come jogging, and one woman walks her lapdog. Anita notices the profusion of shrubs. It would be easy to capture somebody here. Easy to rape somebody, if you wanted to. She herself had sometimes hidden in those bushes, kissing Juan.

There is no sign of Aisling, in the rose arbour, among the peacocks. Anita sees four or five of them, fantails spread, blue and jade and green, with their glinting eyes which she has always found vaguely disconcerting, beautiful but in the manner of beautiful things that seem faintly obscene, that remind you of perversions. Like coral, or the shape of certain orchids.

One peacock walks right up to Anita and seems to be talking to her. Probably hoping she'd have some peanuts. But she has nothing for him. She shudders suddenly and goes to the café. Aisling is not there either.

She is so exhausted by the worry, by the wine, that she sits in the café and drinks a mineral water.

A couple sit at the next table. They are middle-aged, about Anita's age. The woman is slender, with dark fair hair pulled back from her face in a chignon, gold ear-rings, the pared-down summer clothes that fashionable Spaniards favour. The man is Juan. He has put on weight but is instantly recognizable.

The couple order coffee and chat to one another as they wait for it to arrive. Juan is the old lively Juan. He seems to be telling a story of great moment; his voice rises and falls, he waves his hands in the air. Actually, as Anita can hear since he speaks in such a loud voice, he is talking about the visit of a plumber to his house that morning. There is some problem with the water supply. So apparently he owns the family summer house now? Or some other summer house? Anyway, he is still coming here on holiday, as he used to do when he was a young man. Maybe that is not so strange. Anita cannot make out from the conversation whether this woman is his wife or not. He tells the tale of the plumber as if it were a story from the *Odyssey*. The airlocked pipes are a monster with three heads. The plumber is an imposter posing as a dragon slayer. Wouldn't his wife know all about this already? Maybe not. Maybe she has been on the beach all day and now has to get the full story from him. He would tell it with as much panache to a woman he had lived with for twenty years as he would to a stranger, or a new lover he is trying to impress. That's just the way he talks to everyone.

Anita tries to catch his eye but can't, so absorbed in his story is he. Is the woman his wife? She will find out. She finishes her water, leaves the money on the table, and goes up to Juan.

'Hello, Juan?' she says. Her voice sings out across the café.

He breaks off his narrative and looks at her without recognition. The woman eyes her coldly.

'I'm Anita,' she says. 'I knew you years ago. Don't you remember?'

He shakes his head and laughs in an embarrassed way.

'I am afraid there is some mistake,' he says. 'I have never known any woman called Anita.'

Anita stares at his bright blue eyes. There is no mistake about it. He is Juan.

'I worked at the hotel,' she says. 'You were with your mother in your summer house.' What was the name of the summer house? She doesn't remember. Perhaps she never knew, since she never visited it.

He shakes his head, laughs, and turns away, resuming, at a lower volume, his conversation with the other woman.

Anita is stunned. How can he be so rude? Or can he really have totally forgotten her? She walks as fast as she can away from the park, hails the first taxi she sees. In the driver's mirror, she sees herself, with her platinum hair, her treble chin, her ridiculous ear-rings. 'I've turned into Sharon,' she says, aloud, in English. 'What?' asks the chauffeur. 'Nothing,' she says. 'Nada.'

Within minutes she is back in the hotel.

She opens the door of the room without knocking.

What she finds is not the worst thing. Not Marcus and Aisling in bed together. But it is alarming enough. Marcus is sitting on the sofa, in front of the television set. The curtains have been pulled. Aisling is lying down, her head in his lap He is stroking her hair. It's hard to see more in the dim room.

They turn when Anita comes in, but Aisling remains where she is and Marcus makes no attempt to push her away.

They are watching television, watching a bullfight.

'Hi Mum,' says Aisling, in a friendly, warm tone. She sits up, slowly, taking her time. Marcus pats her on the shoulder, in a fatherly gesture. 'Did you have a good walk?'

'Yes,' sings Anita. 'Why yes, I did.'

Why yes, I did. That's not a phrase she ever learned in Cork. It's a phrase from books, or television, and it strikes her that she's never knowingly used it before.

Aisling slips off the sofa and goes to the mini fridge, from which she takes a bottle of water. She turns and asks Marcus and Anita if they want anything. They both shake their heads. Marcus still does not look at Anita, but stares at the television set. Aisling takes her bottle of water and goes back to the sofa, sitting upright now, with several inches of wine-coloured silk between her and her stepfather.

Anita watches the matador circling the bull, his red cloak flapping, his sword poised, his pointed feet dancing, dancing.